Sir Arthur Conan Doyle's
THE ADVENTURES OF
SHERLOCK HOLMES

Other Avon Camelot Books
in the series:

Sir Arthur Conan Doyle's
THE ADVENTURES OF SHERLOCK HOLMES
adapted by
Catherine Edwards Sadler

Sir Arthur Conan Doyle's

THE ADVENTURES OF
SHERLOCK HOLMES

BOOK ONE

A Study in Scarlet
The Red-headed League
The Man with the Twisted Lip

Adapted for young readers by
CATHERINE EDWARDS SADLER

Illustrated by ANDREW GLASS

AN AVON CAMELOT BOOK

SIR ARTHUR CONAN DOYLE'S THE ADVENTURES OF SHERLOCK
HOLMES adapted by Catherine Edwards Sadler is an original publication of Avon
Books. This work has never before appeared in book form.

AVON BOOKS
A division of
The Hearst Corporation
105 Madison Avenue
New York, New York 10016

Table of Contents

Introduction

Sir Arthur Conan Doyle was born in Edinburgh, Scotland, on May 22, 1859. In 1876 he entered the Edinburgh Medical College as a student of medicine. There he met a certain professor named Joseph Bell. Bell enjoyed amusing his students in a most unusual way. He would tell them a patient's medical and personal history before the patient had uttered a single word! He would observe the exact appearance of the patient and note the smallest detail about him: marks on his hands, stains on his clothing, the jewelry he wore. He would observe a tattoo, a new gold chain, a worn hat with unusual stains upon it. From these *observations* he would then make *deductions*. In other words, he would come to conclusions by reasoning in a logical manner. For example, a tattoo and the way a man walked could lead to the deduction that the man had been to sea; a new gold chain could lead to the deduction that he had come into recent wealth. Time and time again Professor Bell's deductions proved correct!

Conan Doyle was intrigued by Professor Bell's skills of observation and deduction. Since his early youth he had been fascinated by the mysterious. He loved mysteries and detective stories. He himself had already tried his hand at writing. Now a new sort of hero began to take shape in Conan Doyle's mind. His hero would be a detective—not just an ordinary detective, though. No, he would be extraordinary . . . a man like Bell who observed the smallest detail. He would take his skills of observation and work them out to an exact science—the science of deduction. "It is all very well to say that a man is clever," Conan Doyle wrote, "but the reader wants to see examples of it—such examples as Bell gave us every day. . . ." So Conan Doyle created just such a clever man, a man who had perfected the skill of observation, turned it into an exact science, and then used it as the basis of his career. His cleverness would be revealed in the extraordinary methods he used to solve his cases and capture his criminals.

Little by little the personality and world of his new character took shape. At last he became the sharp-featured fellow we all know as Mr. Sherlock Holmes. Next Conan Doyle turned his imagination to Holmes' surroundings—those "comfortable rooms in Baker Street"—where the fire was always blazing and where footsteps were always heard on the stair. And then there was Watson, dear old Watson! He was much like Conan Doyle himself, easygoing, typically British, a doctor and a writer. Watson would be Holmes' sidekick, his friend and his chronicler. He would be humble and admiring, always asking Holmes to explain his theories, always ready to go out into the foggy, gaslit streets of London on some mysterious mission. All that remained to create were the adventures themselves.

Taking up his pen in 1886, Conan Doyle set to work on a short novel, or novella as it is sometimes called. He finished *A Study in Scarlet* in just two months. It was the first of sixty Sherlock Holmes stories to come and it began a career for Dr. Arthur Conan Doyle that would eventually win him a knighthood.

Today Holmes is considered one of—if not *the*—most popular fictional heroes of all time. More has been written about this character than any other. Sherlock Holmes societies have been created, plays and movies based on the detective have been made, a castle in Switzerland houses a Sherlock Holmes collection, a tavern in London bears his name and features a reconstruction of his rooms in Baker Street. He has even been poked fun at and been called everything from Picklock Holes to Hemlock Jones!

Why such a fuss over a character who appeared in a series of stories close to a century ago? Elementary, dear reader! He is loved. He is loved for his genius, his coolness, his individuality, and for the safety he represents. For as long as Sherlock Holmes is alive the world is somehow safe. The villains will be outsmarted and good and justice will win out. And so he has been kept alive these hundred years by readers around the globe. And since today we are still in need of just such a clever hero it seems a safe deduction that Mr. Sherlock Holmes—and his dear old Watson—will go on living in these pages for a good many more years to come.

A
Study
in
Scarlet

A Study in Scarlet was the first story featuring Mr. Sherlock Holmes. Conan Doyle's hero was not particularly well-liked at first. Reviewers did not know what to make of his cocky personality and peculiar ways. In fact, when the novella was published in 1887 Sherlock Holmes' future as the first consulting detective looked pretty bleak!

Of course, this was only a temporary situation. Later readers and reviewers would come to love Conan Doyle's creation. They would consider *A Study in Scarlet* a literary classic. For it is here that we have the famous meeting between Dr. Watson and Sherlock Holmes. And it is in *A Study in Scarlet* that Mr. Holmes' unusual "science of deduction" is first explained.

Part One
From the Journal of
Dr. John H. Watson

Chapter 1
Mr. Sherlock Holmes

I, Dr. John H. Watson, studied medicine at the University of London. I received my degree in 1878 and joined an army regiment in India. During the Afghan war I was struck down—first by a bullet and then by fever. I became so weak and thin that I was finally sent back to England to recover my health.

For some time I lived in a private hotel in London. It was very expensive and I soon decided to move to cheaper lodgings. On the very day I made this decision I bumped into an old friend. It was he who told me of Mr. Sherlock Holmes.

"Holmes works in the chemical laboratory at the hospital," my friend Stamford told me. "He was just saying that he has found some nice rooms but that they are too expensive for him. He was considering taking on a roommate."

"By Jove," I cried. "If he really wants to share the apartment and the expense, then I am the very man for him. I should prefer a roommate to living alone."

"You don't know Sherlock Holmes yet," said Stamford. "Perhaps you won't care for him as a constant companion. He is a bit queer in his ideas."

"A medical student, I suppose?" I asked.

"No, I don't think so," Stamford answered. "I'm not quite sure what he's studying. In fact, his studies seem a bit eccentric. He is always amazing his professors by knowing all sorts of extraordinary knowledge."

"Did you ever ask him in what field he wants to work?" I asked.

"No, he isn't an easy man to draw out . . . though he can talk when something interests him."

"I should like to meet him," I said. "I would prefer a studious and quiet roommate."

"He is sure to be at the laboratory. He either avoids the place completely or works there from morning to night. But you mustn't blame me if you don't get along."

"Why shouldn't I get along with him, Stamford? Does he have a terrible temper or strange habits? Now, be straight with me."

"It is hard to say," Stamford said with a laugh. "Holmes is a little too scientific for my tastes. He seems rather cold-blooded. I could imagine him giving a friend a little pinch of poison—not out of meanness, but out of a spirit of inquiry . . . to have an accurate idea of its effects. I think he would take it himself with the same readiness. He appears to have a passion for definite and exact knowledge."

"Very right, too," I added.

"Yes, but it can go too far," Stamford said. "Why, I saw him beat the corpses in the dissecting room! He wanted to see if bruises can be produced after death! Heaven knows what his studies are!"

We found Stamford's curious friend at the laboratory as he said. The lofty room was filled with countless bottles. Broad, low tables were scattered about. On them were test tubes and little Bunsen burners with blue flickering flames. There was only one student in the room. He was bending over a distant table. He seemed totally absorbed in his work. At the sound of our steps he glanced around. On seeing us he sprang to his feet.

"I've found it! I've found it!" he shouted at Stamford. "I have found a foolproof test for detecting the presence of blood!"

Had he discovered a gold mine, he couldn't have been happier.

"Dr. Watson, Mr. Sherlock Holmes," introduced Stamford.

"You have been in Afghanistan, I perceive," said Sherlock Holmes.

"How on earth did you know that?" I asked in astonishment.

"Never mind," said Holmes. "The question now is about blood." He seized my coatsleeve and pulled me toward his work table. "Let us have some fresh blood," he said and pricked his own finger with a long needle. "Now I place this small quantity of blood into a liter of water. You see that the mixture still looks like pure water. The proportion of blood to water cannot be more than one in a million." As he spoke, he threw a few white crystals into the water and then added some drops of a clear fluid. In an instant the contents turned a dull color. A brownish dust settled at the bottom of the jar.

"Ha! Ha!" he cried, clapping his hands. He looked as delighted as a child with a new toy. "The change in color

shows there is blood in the water. The old tests were clumsy and inaccurate. The blood always had to be fresh. My test seems to work whether the blood is old or new. Had it been invented earlier, many criminals would not have escaped punishment."

"Indeed!" I murmured.

"Criminal cases always seem to hinge on one point. A man is usually suspected of a crime months after it has been committed. His clothes are examined. Brownish stains are discovered on them. Are they bloodstains, or mud stains, or rust stains, or fruit stains? These are the questions which have puzzled many an expert—and why? Because there was no reliable test. But now we have Sherlock Holmes' test. There will no longer be any difficulty."

His eyes glittered as he spoke. He put his hand over his heart and bowed to some imaginary, applauding audience.

"You are to be congratulated," I remarked.

"There was the case of Van Bischoff at Frankfort last year. He would certainly have hung had this test been in existence. Then there was Mason of Bradford and the notorious Mulles and Lefevre of Montpellier and Samson of New Orleans. I could name a score of cases in which my test would have proven someone's guilt."

"You seem to be a walking calendar of crime," said Stamford with a laugh. "You might start a paper along those lines. You could call it *Police News of the Past.*"

"And very interesting reading it would make," replied Holmes.

"We came here on business," said Stamford. He sat down on a three-legged stool. He pushed another in my direction with his foot. "My friend here wants to find new lodgings. You were complaining that you needed a roommate—so I thought I'd bring you two together."

Sherlock Holmes seemed delighted. "I have my eye on some comfortable rooms in Baker Street," he said. "You don't mind the smell of strong tobacco, I hope?"

"I smoke myself," I answered.

"I generally have chemicals about and sometimes perform experiments. Would that annoy you?"

"By no means."

"Let me see—what are my other shortcomings? I get down in the dumps at times and don't open my mouth for days on end. You must not think I am sulky when I do that. Just leave me alone and I'll soon be right. What have you to confess now? It's best for two fellows to know the worst about each other before they live together."

I laughed at this cross-examination. "I object to arguments because my nerves are shaky. I get up at ungodly hours and am extremely lazy," I said. "I have another set of faults when I am well, but those are the main ones at present."

"Do you consider violin-playing a source of arguments?" Holmes asked anxiously.

"It depends on the player," I answered. "A well-played violin is a treat for the gods. A badly played one—"

"Oh, that's all right," he cried, with a merry laugh. "I think we may consider the thing settled . . . if the rooms are agreeable to you."

"When shall we see them?"

"Call for me here at noon tomorrow. We'll see the rooms and settle everything then," he answered. He turned back to his experiments and soon seemed to forget we were even there.

"By the way," I later asked Stamford, "how did he know that I was in Afghanistan?"

"Only Sherlock Holmes can answer that!" Stamford replied.

We said goodbye and I strolled back to my hotel. I was very much interested in my mysterious new acquaintance, Mr. Sherlock Holmes.

Chapter 2
The Science of Deduction

We met the next day as agreed and inspected the rooms at No. 221B Baker Street. They consisted of a couple of comfortable bedrooms and a large, airy, sitting room. The sitting room was cheerfully furnished and well-lit by two broad windows. We rented the apartment on the spot. That very evening I moved my things from the hotel. Sherlock Holmes moved in the following morning. At first we busied ourselves with unpacking, but gradually we began to settle in.

Holmes was certainly not a difficult man to live with. He was quiet in his ways and his habits were regular. It was rare for him to be up after 10 at night. He always breakfasted early and was usually out before I rose in the morning. Sometimes he spent his day at the chemical laboratory, sometimes in the dissecting rooms, and occasionally in walks about the city.

As the weeks passed, I found myself more and more interested in my new roommate. Even his appearance was fascinating to me. He was over six feet tall and so lean that he appeared even taller. His nose was hawklike and his eyes were sharp and piercing. His chin was strong and square. His hands were always blotted with ink and stained with chemicals.

For the life of me, I could not figure out what his occupation was. He knew the most exact details on certain subjects. Yet, on other subjects, he was totally ignorant. I was utterly shocked, for example, to find out that he knew nothing of the solar system. Imagine someone living in this 19th Century and not knowing that the earth traveled around the sun!

"You appear to be astonished," he said. He smiled at my surprise. "I consider man's mind like an empty attic. A fool takes in all the things he comes across. The attic becomes cluttered. When he needs some piece of information he cannot find it. Now, the smart man is very careful as to what he takes into his brain-attic. He takes in only what he can use. It is a mistake to think the little brain-attic has elastic walls. At some point it becomes too full, then you must forget something you already know for each new piece of knowledge you take in. Therefore it is of the highest importance not to have useless information elbowing out useful information."

"But the solar system!" I protested.

"What is it to me?" he interrupted. "You say that we go around the sun. If we went around the moon it wouldn't make any difference to me or my work."

I was about to ask him what that work might be, but something told me not to. Instead I tried to figure it out on my own. He had said that he only knew knowledge useful to his work. I tried to think about what it was he knew well. I even took a pencil and made a list:

SHERLOCK HOLMES
1. knowledge of literature—none
2. knowledge of philosophy—none
3. knowledge of astronomy—none
4. knowledge of politics—little
5. knowledge of botany—limited
   (knows about poisons—knows nothing of practical gardening)
6. knowledge of geology—practical but limited
   (tells at a glance different soils from each other. After walks has shown me splashes from his trousers and told me by their color and consistency from what part of London they came)
7. knowledge of chemistry—excellent
8. knowledge of anatomy—accurate
9. knowledge of sensational literature—immense
   (he appears to know every crime committed in the century)
10. plays violin well
11. is an excellent boxer and swordsman
12. has a good knowledge of British law

When I got this far I threw my list into the fire. What could his profession be?

It was not long, however, before I found out. During our first weeks together we had few callers. I was beginning to think Sherlock had as few friends as I. I soon discovered that I was wrong. He had many different types of acquaintances. There was a little rat-faced man called Mr. Lestrade. He came three or four times a week. One morning a fashionably dressed girl visited for half an hour or more. The same afternoon a gray-haired visitor arrived who looked like a peddler of sorts. Another time a white-haired gentleman had an interview with my companion. Once a railway porter visited. Each time Sherlock Holmes begged for the use of the sitting room. "I have to use the room as a place of business," he would say. "These people are my clients."

It was on the 4th of March that I found out what type of clients they were. I rose earlier than usual. Sherlock had not yet finished his breakfast. I ordered mine and looked through a magazine while I waited for it to arrive. One of the articles had been marked in pencil. I began to read it.

It was entitled "The Book of Life." It was about how much one can learn through observation. The writer claimed that he could read one's inmost thoughts by an expression . . . a twitch of a muscle or the glance of an eye. "By a man's fingernails, by his coatsleeve, by his trouserknees, by his shirtcuff, a man's history and trade is plainly revealed."

"I never read such rubbish in my life!" I cried, slapping down the magazine.

"What is it?" Sherlock asked.

"Why, this article," I said. I pointed with my eggspoon to the magazine. "I see you have read it as it is marked. I should like to see the author aboard a train. I would bet a thousand to one that he could not pick the trades of his fellow travelers."

"You would lose your money," Holmes remarked. "As for the article, I wrote it myself."

"You!"

"Yes, I enjoy both observation and deduction. In fact, I depend upon both for my living."

"How?" I asked at last.

"Well, I have a trade all my own. I suppose I am the only one in the world. I'm a consulting detective. Here in London we have lots of government detectives and lots of private detectives. When these fellows have problems with a case they come to me. I manage to put them on the right scent. They lay all the evidence before me. I usually can set them straight. My knowledge of the history of crime is a great help. There is a strong family resemblance between crimes. If you have all the details of one thousand crimes at your fingertips, you can usually unravel the one thousand and first. Lestrade is a well-known detective. He was having trouble with a forgery case and came to me for help."

"And these other people?"

"They are all people in trouble. I listen to their stories, they listen to my comments, and then I pocket my fee."

"But do you mean to say," I said, "that you can unravel something which others can make nothing of? Even when they have all the facts? Without ever leaving this room?"

"Quite so," Sherlock Holmes said, "I have a kind of intuition that way. Now and again a case turns up which is a little more complex. Then I have to bustle about and see things with my own eyes. Observation is second nature to me. For example, you appeared surprised when I told you that you had been in Afghanistan."

"No doubt you were told," I commented.

"Nothing of the sort. I deduced it in a matter of seconds. My reasoning was as follows: Here is a gentleman of a medical type. But he has the air of a military man. Clearly an army doctor. He has just come from the tropics. His face is dark but it is not his natural color as his wrists are pale. His worn face tells me that he has undergone hardship and sickness. His left arm has been injured. He holds it in a stiff and unnatural way. Then I asked myself where in the tropics an English army doctor could have seen much hardship and got his arm wounded. Clearly in Afghanistan. I then remarked that you had been there and you were astonished."

"It is simple enough as you explain it," I said. I walked over to the window and looked out. A man was walking across the street. "I wonder what that fellow is looking for," I commented. He was a plainly dressed man. He was looking anxiously at the building numbers. In his hand was a large blue envelope.

Sherlock walked over to the window and stared out. "You mean the retired marine sergeant?"

"What conceit!" I thought to myself. "He knows I cannot check his guess."

Suddenly the man saw the number on our door and ran across the street. We heard a loud knock, and the housekeeper opening the door.

"For Mr. Sherlock Holmes," he told her. In a moment he was up the stairs and standing before us. He handed my friend the letter.

Here was my opportunity to take the conceit out of Mr. Sherlock Holmes.

"May I ask you what your trade is?" I said to the messenger.

"I am retired now," he said. "But I used to be a marine sergeant." He clicked his heels together, raised his hand in a salute and left.

Chapter 3
The Brixton Road Mystery

"How in the world did you deduce that?" I asked Holmes.

"Deduce what?" he asked, looking up from his note.

"Why, that he was a retired marine sergeant."

"Even across the street, I could see a great blue anchor tattooed on the back of his hand. That smacked of the sea. Yet he had a military manner. There we have the marine. And he had a certain air of command. You must have observed the way in which he held his head and swung his cane. He looked like a steady, respectable, middle-aged man. All facts that led me to believe he was a sergeant."

"Wonderful," I exclaimed in admiration.

"Commonplace," replied Holmes. "Look at this." He handed me the note.

"Why," I cried as I read it. "This is terrible."

"It does seem to be a little out of the ordinary," he

remarked calmly. "Would you mind reading it to me aloud?"

The letter said:

Dear Mr. Sherlock Holmes,

A man was killed last night on Brixton Road. At two in the morning one of our policemen spotted a light in a vacant house there. Thinking something was wrong, he tried the door. It was open. In the front room he discovered the body of a gentleman. The business card in his pocket read: "Enoch J. Drebber, Cleveland, Ohio, U.S.A." There was no robbery, nor is there any evidence as to the cause of death. There are marks of blood in the room, but there is no wound on the body. We do not know how the man entered the house. Indeed the entire affair is a mystery. Your assistance in this would be greatly appreciated. If you come around before 12 noon, you will find me there. I have ordered everything left exactly as it was found.

Yours Faithfully,
Tobias Gregson

"Gregson is the smartest detective working at Scotland Yard, though that is not saying much. He and Lestrade lack that special genius it takes to be a true detective. Still, they are very jealous of each other and each is always trying to better the other. It is quite a comedy. If both are working on this case, it could be amusing!"

I was amazed at the calm way in which Sherlock rattled on. "Surely there is not a moment to lose," I cried. "Shall I go and order you a cab?"

"I'm not sure that I shall go," Holmes responded.

"Why, this is just the chance you've been waiting for!"

"Supposing I unravel the whole matter," said Holmes. "You may be sure Lestrade and Co. will claim the credit. They will not admit an unofficial person solved the case when they could not. How would it look for Scotland Yard? No, they will claim the credit and there will be nothing I can do."

"But he begs you to help him."

"Yes. He needs my talent and admits it to me. But he would rather cut his tongue out than admit it to anyone else. However, we may as well go and have a look. It could prove interesting and it's always fun to show them how it should be done. Not that they learn." Holmes put on his overcoat and gathered up his tools. "Get your hat," he added.

"You wish me to come?" I asked in a surprised voice.

"Yes, if you have nothing better to do."

A moment later we were both in a hansom cab driving furiously toward Brixton Road.

It was a dark, cloudy night. A veil of fog hung thick over London's rooftops. We were soon at the scene of the crime. A FOR RENT sign hung in the window. A small walled-in garden and a claylike pathway separated the house from the street. The ground was wet and sloppy from that night's rain.

I had thought Holmes would rush into the house and plunge into the mystery at hand. But no, he gazed leisurely at the ground, the sky, the opposite houses. He walked up and down the pathway and looked at the grass growing along its edge. He seemed particularly interested in the maze of footprints in the clayey soil.

At the door we were met by a tall, white-faced man. He held a notebook in his hand. It was Gregson of Scotland Yard.

"It is kind of you to come," he told Holmes. "Everything has been left untouched."

"Except that!" my friend answered, pointing to the pathway. "If a herd of buffaloes passed along, there could be no greater mess! No doubt you have already drawn your conclusions about the case, Gregson, and that is why you no longer needed to preserve the evidence! Otherwise, I am sure you would not have permitted such a thing."

"I have had so much to do inside the house," the detective said nervously. "My colleague, Mr. Lestrade, is here. I expected him to look after the grounds."

Holmes glanced at me and raised his eyebrows. "With two such men as yourself and Lestrade handling the case, there is not much for a third person to find out," he said sarcastically.

Gregson rubbed his hands in a self-satisfied way. "I think we have done all that can be done," he answered. "It's a queer case, though, and I knew your taste for such things."

"Did you come here in a cab?" asked Sherlock Holmes.

"No, sir," answered Gregson.

"Nor Lestrade?"

"No."

"Then let us go and look at the room," Holmes said, and strode into the house. He was followed by an astonished Mr. Gregson.

A short passage led to the kitchen and offices. A door to the right led to the front room. It was here that the body had been found. It was a large square room. A glaring wallpaper was on the walls. Here and there strips hung down and showed the yellow plaster beneath. Opposite the door was a mantelpiece. On it was stuck the stump of a red wax candle. A body lay motionless on the floor. His eyes stared up at the ceiling. The dead man seemed forty-three or four years of age, middle-sized and broad-shouldered, with curly black hair and a short, stubby beard. He was well dressed. A new top hat lay beside him. His hands were clenched and his arms and legs were oddly twisted. On his face was an expression of utter horror and hatred.

Detective Lestrade was standing at the doorway.

"This case will make a stir," he remarked. "It beats anything I have ever seen."

"There are no clues," added Gregson.

"None at all," chimed in Lestrade.

Sherlock Holmes approached the body. He kneeled down and examined it closely. "You are sure that there is no wound?" he asked, pointing to splashes of blood on the floor.

"Positive!" cried both detectives.

"Then this blood must belong to a second individual—probably the murderer . . . if murder has been committed. It reminds me of the death of Van Jansen, in Utrecht, in '34. Do you remember the case, Gregson?"

"No, sir."

"Read about it—you really should. There is nothing new under the sun. It has all been done before."

As he spoke his fingers flew in all directions, feeling, pressing, unbuttoning, examining. Finally Sherlock sniffed the dead man's lips and glanced at the soles of his patent leather boots.

"Has he been moved at all?" Holmes asked.

"No more than was necessary for the purpose of our examination."

"You can take him to the mortuary now," Holmes said. "There is nothing more to be learned."

Gregson had four men and a stretcher standing by. They were now called in. Just as the men were raising the body, a ring tinkled down and rolled across the floor. Lestrade grabbed it. He stared at it with mystified eyes.

"There's been a woman here!" he cried. "It's a woman's wedding ring!" He held it out on the palm of his hand. We all gathered around him and gazed at it. There could be no doubt. The ring had once been worn by a bride.

"This complicates matters," said Gregson. "Heaven knows, they were complicated before."

"You're sure it doesn't simplify them?" observed Holmes. "There's nothing to be learned by staring at it. What did you find in his pockets?"

"We have it all here," said Gregson, pointing to a small pile of objects. "A gold watch, No. 97163 by Barraud of London; a gold Albert Chain, very heavy and solid; a gold ring; a gold pin in the shape of a bull's head with rubies for eyes; a Russian leather cardcase with the name Enoch J. Drebber on it; no wallet but loose money; a book with the name Joseph Stangerson written on it; and two letters—one addressed to E. J. Drebber and one to Joseph Stangerson."

"At what address?"

"American Exchange, Strand—to be picked up. Both letters are from the Guion Steamship Company. They are about boat departures to New York from Liverpool. It appears that this unfortunate man was about to return to New York."

"Have you made inquiries as to who Stangerson was?"

"I did it at once, sir," said Gregson. "I placed an advertisement in all the newspapers and one of my men has gone to the American Exchange. He has not yet returned."

"Have you telegraphed Cleveland?"

"This morning."

"How did you word your inquiries?"

"We simply detailed the circumstances and said that we should be glad of any information which could help us," answered Gregson.

"You didn't ask for particulars on any crucial points?"

"I asked about Stangerson."

"Nothing else? Is there no circumstance on which the whole case appears to hinge? Will you not telegraph again?" Holmes asked.

"I have said all I have to say," said an offended Gregson.

Sherlock Holmes chuckled to himself. Just then Lestrade appeared.

"Mr. Gregson," he said, "I have just made a discovery of the highest importance. One which would have been overlooked had I not made a careful examination of the walls."

The little man's eyes sparkled as he spoke. He was very much pleased to have scored a point against his colleague.

"Come here," he said, bustling back into the room. "Now stand there!"

He struck a match on his boot and held it up against the wall.

"Look at that!" he said triumphantly.

Written on the wall in blood was a single word:

RACHE

"What do you think of that?" cried the detective. "This was overlooked because it is the darkest corner of the room. No one thought to look here. The murderer has written it with his or her own blood. See this smear where it had trickled down the wall! So much for the idea of suicide anyway. Why was that corner chosen to write it on? I will tell you. See that candle on the mantelpiece? It was lit at the time. If it was lit, this corner of the room would be the brightest instead of the darkest portion of the wall."

"And what does it mean now that you *have* found it?" asked Gregson.

"Mean? Why, it means that the writer was about to write the female name Rachel—but was disturbed before he or she had time to finish. You mark my words. When this case is cleared up, you will find that a woman named Rachel had something to do with it." With that Sherlock Holmes burst into laughter.

"It's all very well for you to laugh, Mr. Sherlock Holmes. You may be very smart and clever. But the old hound is the best when all is said and done."

"You certainly have the credit for being the first to discover this," said Holmes. "I have not had time to examine this room yet. With your permission I shall do so now."

Sherlock whipped out of his pocket a tape measure and a large magnifying glass. He trotted about the room, sometimes stopping, sometimes kneeling, once lying flat on his face. As he worked he chattered away under his breath. As I watched him I was reminded of a well-trained foxhound. For twenty minutes he examined and measured the room. In one place he even gathered up a little pile of gray dust and placed the ashes in an envelope. Finally, he examined the word on the wall. He looked at every letter with his magnifying glass.

"What do you think of it, sir?" the detectives asked.

"You are doing so well; I hate to interfere," he said. "Let me know how your investigations go. I shall be happy to give you any help I can. In the meantime, I should like to speak to the policeman who found the body. Can you give me his name and address?"

Lestrade glanced at his notebook. "John Rance," he said. "He is off-duty now. You will find him at 46 Audley Court, Kennington Park Gate."

Holmes took note of the address.

"Come along, Doctor," he said. "We shall go and look him up." Then he turned to the detectives. "I'll tell you one thing which may help in the case. There has been a murder. The murderer was a man. He was over 6 feet tall, was in the prime of his life, had small feet for his height, wore coarse, square-toed boots, and smoked an imported cigar. He came here with his victim in a four-wheeled cab. The cab was drawn by a horse with three old shoes and one new one on his foreleg. Most likely the murderer had a ruddy face and the fingernails of his right hand were remarkably long."

Lestrade and Gregson glanced at each other in disbelief.

"If this man was murdered, how was it done?" asked Lestrade.

"Poison," replied Sherlock Holmes curtly. He started to walk away. "One other thing, Lestrade," he added, turning around, " 'RACHE' is the German word for 'revenge.' So don't waste your time looking for Miss Rachel."

With that he walked out the door, leaving Lestrade and Gregson standing open-mouthed in the room.

Chapter 4
What John Rance Had to Tell

We left Brixton Road at one o'clock in the afternoon. We went straight to the nearest telegraph office where Sherlock sent a long telegram. He then hailed a taxi and gave the driver the policeman's address.

"There is nothing like firsthand evidence," Sherlock remarked in the cab. "In fact, my mind is already made up about the case. Still, we might as well learn everything there is to know."

"You amaze me, Holmes," said I. "Surely you aren't as positive about the facts as you seemed to be back at the house."

"There's no room for a mistake," he answered. "It is a matter of observation. The first thing I observed was that a cab's wheels had made two ruts in the soil. Now, up to last night, we had no rain for a week. Thus, those ruts *must* have been made last night. I could also see the marks of the horse's shoes. One was much clearer than the others. It was obviously a newer shoe. Now, Gregson told us that no cabs had arrived in the morning. We can therefore conclude that it arrived during the night—and brought the murderer and his victim."

"That seems simple enough," said I. "But how did you know about the murderer's height?"

"The height of a man can usually be told from the length of his stride. His footprints were in the clay outside and on the dust within. Thus it was an easy matter to figure his height. I even had a way to check my calculation. When a man writes on the wall, his instinct is to write above eye level. Now, the German word was written just over six feet from the ground. It was child's play."

"And his age?" I asked.

"Well, if a man can stride four and a half feet without the smallest effort, he can't be too old. That was the length of the puddle on the garden walk. The footprints showed that Patent-leather boots walked around it and Square-toes hopped over it. There is no mystery about it at all. Does anything else puzzle you?"

"What about the fingernails and the cigar?"

"The writing on the wall was done with a man's

forefinger dipped in blood. My magnifying glass showed that the plaster was scratched. It would not have been had his nails been trimmed. I gathered up some scattered ash from the floor. It was dark and flaky—definitely that of a cigar."

"And the flushed face?" I asked.

"Ah, that was my most daring deduction. But I have no doubt that I am right. Still, I cannot tell you how I deduced it quite yet."

I passed my hand over my brow. "My head is in a whirl," I remarked. "The more one thinks about this case, the more mysterious it becomes! Why did these two men go to an empty house? What has become of the cabman who drove them? How could one man force the other to take poison? Where did the blood come from? What was the object of the murder? It was obviously not robbery. Where did the woman's ring come from? Above all, why did the second man write the German word RACHE on the wall?"

Sherlock Holmes smiled approvingly.

"You sum up the difficulties of this case well. There is still much to be discovered. But as I said, I have made up my mind about the main facts. As to the writing on the wall, it was merely a means of getting us off the true scent. But I am not going to tell you much more about the case. A magician does not get credit once he has explained his tricks. If I show you too much of my method of working, you'll come to the conclusion that I am a very ordinary individual after all."

"I shall never do that," I answered. "You have brought detection as near to an exact science as it will ever be."

My companion flushed with pleasure at my words.

"I'll tell you one other thing," he said. "Patent-leather boots and Square-toes came in the same cab. They walked down the pathway as friendly as can be . . . probably arm-in-arm. When they got inside they paced up and down the room—rather, Patent-leather boots stood while Square-toes walked up and down. I could read all that in the dust. I could also read that as he walked he grew more and more excited. That is shown by the increased length of his strides. No doubt, he was talking all the while and working himself up into a fury. Then the tragedy occurred. Now I've told you as much as I know myself. The rest is guesswork. We have a good basis, however, on which to start." Just then the cab came to a stop and our cabman said, "That's Audley Court in there." He was pointing to a dark alleyway.

Audley Court was not in the best part of town. We picked our way through groups of dirty children and lines of discolored linen until we came to number 46. On the door was the name "RANCE." On asking, we learned that the constable was in bed. We were shown into a little front parlor and told to wait.

John Rance soon appeared. "I made my report at the office," he said irritably.

Holmes took a coin from his pocket. "We would like to hear it from your own lips."

"I shall be most happy to tell you anything I can," the policeman answered, his eyes on the little golden coin.

Rance sat himself down on the sofa. "I'll tell it to you from the beginning. My worktime is from ten at night to six in the morning. At eleven there was a fight at the White Hart Tavern, but other than that all was quiet on the beat. At one o'clock it began to rain. I met a fellow policeman, Harry Murcher, and we stood together talking. At about two, or a little after, I thought I would take a look around and see that all was right on Brixton Road. I didn't meet a soul as I walked, though a cab or two went past me. I strolled down the street. The glint of a light caught my eye. I knew the house was vacant. I went to the door and pushed it open. All was quiet inside, so I went to where the light was burning. A candle was flickering on the mantelpiece—a red wax one. By its light I saw—"

"Yes, I know what you saw. You walked around the room several times, and you knelt down by the body, and then you walked through and tried the kitchen door, and then—"

John Rance sprang to his feet. "Where were you hiding to see all that?" he cried. "It seems to me that you know a great deal more than you should!"

Holmes laughed and threw his business card across the table. "Don't go arresting me for murder," he said. "I am working with Mr. Lestrade and Mr. Gregson. Go on. What did you do next?"

Rance sat down again. "I went back to the gate and blew my whistle. That brought Murcher and two more policemen."

"Was the street empty?"

"Well it was, at least for anyone that could be of any use."

"What do you mean?"

The policeman's features broadened into a grin. "There was a drunk. He was at the gate when I came out of the house. He was leaning on the railings and singing at the top of his lungs. He couldn't stand, far less help."

"What sort of man was he?" asked Sherlock Holmes.

John Rance appeared annoyed at the question. "He was a drunk. If we hadn't been so busy, we'd have taken him to the police station."

"His face—his dress—didn't you notice them?" Holmes broke in impatiently.

"I should think I did. Me and Murcher had to prop him up. He was a long chap with a red face. He wore a muffler around his chin—"

"That will do," cried Holmes. "What became of him?"

"We'd enough to do without looking after him," the policeman said. "I'm sure he found his way home."

"How was he dressed?"

"He wore a brown overcoat."

"Had he a whip in his hand?"

"A whip?—No."

"He must have left it behind," muttered Holmes. "You didn't happen to see or hear a cab after that?"

"No."

"There's your coin," Sherlock said. He stood up and took his hat. "Rance, I am afraid you will never rise in your job. You might have gained a sergeant's stripes last night. That drunk holds the clue to this mystery. He is the very man we are seeking. But there is no use arguing about it now. Come along, Doctor."

"The blundering fool!" Holmes said outside. "Just to think of his having the man and letting him go!"

"I am still in the dark," I said. "The 'drunk' did sound like your idea of the second man. But why should he come back to the scene of the crime? That is not the way of criminals."

"The ring, man, the ring. That was what he came back for. I shall capture him, Doctor—I shall have him. We may have to use the ring as bait. I must thank you for it all. I might not have gone to the house but for you. And then I should have missed the finest study in crime I have ever come across . . . a study in scarlet. There's a scarlet thread of murder running through this case, at the moment it is all tangled up. But it is my duty to unravel it."

Chapter 5
Our Advertisement
Brings a Visitor

Our busy morning tired me. I spent the afternoon trying to sleep. But thoughts of the murdered man and his strange death kept me awake. Every time I closed my eyes I could see the victim's face. There was something evil about it. And, there were all the facts of the case to think of. Sherlock seemed to think that the man had died of poison. I remembered how he had sniffed his lips. But whose blood was on the floor? There were no signs of a struggle. There was no weapon with which the victim could have wounded the other man. I felt sure Holmes had already formed a theory which explained all the facts. But I could not figure out what that theory might be.

Holmes had spent the afternoon out. Dinner was

already on the table when he returned. "What's the matter?" he asked. "You're not looking quite yourself. This affair has upset you."

"To tell the truth it has," I said.

"Have you seen the evening paper?"

"No," I answered.

"It gives a fairly good account of the affair. It does not mention the fact that a woman's wedding ring was found. But, it's just as well."

"Why?"

"Look at this advertisement," he answered. "I had one sent to every paper."

He threw the paper across to me. It was the first announcement in the "Found" column:

A PLAIN GOLD WEDDING RING FOUND ON BRIXTON ROAD. APPLY DR. WATSON, 221B BAKER STREET, BETWEEN EIGHT AND NINE THIS EVENING.

"Excuse my using your name. I was afraid someone might recognize mine."

"That's all right. But suppose someone does answer the advertisement. I have no ring."

"Oh, yes you have," Sherlock said, handing me one. "This will do very well. It is almost the same."

"And who do you expect will answer the advertisement?"

"Why, the man in the brown coat—our friend with the flushed face and square toes. He will send a friend if he doesn't come himself."

"Wouldn't he consider it too dangerous?" I asked.

"Not at all. If my view of the case is correct—and I have every reason to believe it is—this man would risk anything rather than lose that ring. I believe he dropped it while leaning over Drebber's body. He must not have missed it at the time. He discovered his loss later and hurried back to the house. But the police were already there because he had left the candle burning. He had to pretend he was drunk so that they would not suspect him. Now put yourself in the man's place. He was not sure *where* the ring was lost. He could have lost it *after* he left the house. What if he had? How could he find it? He would read the Lost and Found section of the newspaper. His eye would see our advertisement. He would be overjoyed. Why should he fear a trap? There was no connection between a lost wedding ring and a murder. He would come. He will come. You shall see him within an hour."

"And then?" I asked.

"Oh, you can leave me to deal with him then. Have you a gun?" Sherlock asked.

"I have my old army revolver and a few bullets."

"You had better clean the gun and load it. He will be a desperate man. It is best to be ready for anything."

I went to my bedroom and followed his advice. When I returned he said, "The plot thickens, I have just had an answer to my American telegram. My view of the case was correct."

"And that is—?"

Sherlock did not answer. He asked me to put my pistol in my pocket. "He will probably be here in a few minutes," he added. "Open the door slightly. That will do. Now put the key on the inside." As he spoke there was a sharp ring at the bell. Sherlock Holmes rose softly and moved his chair in the direction of the door. We heard the housekeeper pass along the hall and the sharp click of the latch as she opened it.

"Does Dr. Watson live here?" asked a clear but rather harsh voice. We could not hear her reply, but we soon heard slow, uncertain steps on the stairs. There was a feeble tap at the door.

"Come in," I cried.

A very old and wrinkled woman hobbled into the apartment. She appeared dazzled by the sudden blaze of light. She curtseyed and stood blinking at us with bleary eyes. I looked over at Sherlock. He looked thunderstruck.

The old woman drew out the evening paper. She pointed to our advertisement.

"The ring belongs to my daughter Sally," she said. "She was married a year ago. Her husband is a sailor and at sea. When he comes home and finds she lost her ring he'll be plenty mad. Last night she went to the circus with—"

"Is that her ring?" I interrupted.

"The Lord be thanked!" cried the woman. "Sally will be a happy woman tonight. That's the ring."

"And what is your address?"

"13 Duncan Street. A long way from here."

"Brixton Road isn't near Duncan Street at all," said Holmes sharply.

The old woman turned around and looked at him with her little red-rimmed eyes. "The gentleman asked my address. Sally lives at 3 Mayfield Place."

"And your name is—?"

"My name is Sawyer—hers is Dennis," she answered.

Sherlock nodded for me to give the old woman the ring. "Here is your ring," I told her. "It clearly belongs to your daughter. I am glad to return it to its rightful owner."

The woman mumbled blessings at us. She put the ring in her pocket and shuffled down the stairs. Sherlock Holmes sprang to his feet the moment she was gone. He rushed into his room. When he returned a few seconds later, he had on his coat and muffler. "I'll follow her," he said hurriedly. "She must be an accomplice. She will lead me to him. Wait up for me."

I rushed to the window. The woman was walking feebly down the street. Sherlock was following some paces behind. "Either his whole theory is incorrect," I thought to myself, "or else she will lead him to the heart of this mystery."

It was close to twelve o'clock before Sherlock returned. I could tell by his face that he had been unsuccessful. "I would not let Lestrade and Gregson know about this little adventure for anything. Not after the way I joked with them!"

"What is it?" I asked.

"The woman had gone a little way when she began to limp as if her feet were sore. She hailed a cab. I got close enough to hear the address. 'Drive to 13 Duncan Street,' she told the driver and got into the cab. 'This begins to look genuine,' I thought. I jumped onto the back of the cab. Well, just before we reached our destination I jumped off and strolled down the street in an easy, lounging way. I saw the cab pull up. But when the driver opened the door no one came out. There was no sign or trace of his passenger or his fare! On inquiring at No. 13 I found that the house belonged to a Mr. Keswick. He had never heard of either a Sawyer or a Dennis."

"You don't mean to say," I said in amazement, "that that old, tottering woman was able to get out of the cab while it was moving—without either you or the driver seeing her?"

"Old woman be damned!" said Sherlock Holmes. "We were the old women to be taken in. It must have been a young man—a very fit one who was also an excellent actor. His getup was perfect. No doubt, he saw that he was followed and so gave me the slip. Now, Doctor, you look tired. Take my advice and turn in."

I left Holmes seated in front of the fire. I heard him playing his violin, long into the night. He was pondering over the strange mystery he had chosen to solve.

Chapter 6
Tobias Gregson Shows
What He Can Do

The next day the papers were full of the "Brixton Mystery," as they called it. Some of the information they reported was new to me. It seemed that the dead man was an American gentleman who had been staying in London for some weeks. He and his secretary, Mr. Joseph Stangerson, were living at the boarding house of a

Madame Charpentier. The two left the boarding house on Tuesday. They told their landlady that they were going to the train station to catch the Liverpool express. They were even seen on the train platform. Nothing more was known of them until Mr. Drebber's body was discovered in the empty house on Brixton Road. Mr. Stangerson's whereabouts, they reported, were still unknown. The newspapers went on to comment that they were glad that Mr. Gregson and Mr. Lestrade of Scotland Yard were working on the case. They were confident the two detectives would soon solve the case.

"I told you that Lestrade and Gregson would receive the credit for this case," commented Sherlock.

"That depends on how it turns out," I said.

"Oh bless you, it doesn't matter in the least. If the man is caught it will be on account of their work; if he escapes, it will be in spite of it. I can't win."

At that moment there came the pattering of many steps in the hall.

"It's the Baker Street division of the detective police force," said Holmes gravely. As he spoke six dirty children rushed into the room.

"'Tention!" cried Holmes, in a sharp tone. All six stood in line. "In future you shall send up Wiggins to report. The rest of you must wait in the street. Have you found it, Wiggins?"

"No, sir, we ain't," said one of the youths.

"I hardly expected you would. You must keep on until you do," said Holmes. "Here are your wages." He handed each of them a coin. "Now, off you go and come back with a better report next time."

He waved his hand and they scampered away.

"The mere sight of an official-looking person seals men's lips," he told me. "These youngsters can go everywhere and hear everything."

"Do you have them working on the Brixton case?" I asked.

"Yes. There is something I want to find out. Oh, look. Here comes Gregson now. He must have some news."

There was a violent peal of the bell. A few seconds later the fair-haired detective was up the stairs and in our sitting room.

"My dear fellow," he cried, shaking Holmes' hand, "congratulate me! I have cleared up the case!"

"Do you mean that you are on the right track?" asked Holmes.

"The right track! Why, sir, we have the murderer under lock and key."

"And his name is?"

"Arthur Charpentier, sub-lieutenant in Her Majesty's navy," cried Gregson. He rubbed his fat hands and puffed out his chest proudly.

Holmes gave a sigh of relief and smiled.

"Take a seat and try one of these cigars," he said. "We are anxious to know how you managed it. Will you have some whiskey and water?"

"I don't mind if I do," the detective answered. "I am worn out from my work. Mental work. You will appreciate that, Mr. Sherlock Holmes. We are both brain-workers."

"You do me too much honor," said Holmes gravely. "Let us hear how you did it."

"The fun of it is, that fool Lestrade thinks he is so smart and yet has gone off on the wrong track. He is after the secretary, Stangerson. But Stangerson had no more to do with the crime than an unborn babe. No doubt he has caught him by now!"

The idea tickled Gregson so much that he laughed until he choked.

"And how did you get your clue?" Holmes asked.

"Ah, I'll tell you all about it. Of course, Dr. Watson, this is strictly between ourselves. The first thing to find out was where Drebber lived. Some people would have waited for their advertisements to be answered. Others would have waited for someone to step forward with information. But that is not Tobias Gregson's way of going to work. You remember the hat beside the dead man?"

"Yes," said Holmes, "by John Underwood and Sons, 129 Camberwell Road."

Gregson looked crestfallen.

"I had no idea you noticed that," he said. "Have you been there?"

"No."

"Ha!" cried Gregson, in a relieved voice. "Well, I went to Underwood and asked him if he had sold a hat of that size and description. He looked over his books and found it at once. He had sent it to Mr. Drebber, Charpentier's Boarding House, Torquay Terrace. Thus I got his address."

"Smart—very smart!" murmured Sherlock Holmes.

"I next called on Madame Charpentier," continued the detective. "I found her very pale and distressed. Her daughter was in the room too. Her eyes were red and she trembled when I spoke to her. That didn't escape my notice. I began to smell a rat. You must know the feeling, Mr. Holmes, when you come upon the right scent—a kind of thrill in your nerves. 'Have you heard of the mysterious death of your late boarder, Mr. Enoch Drebber of Cleveland?' I asked.

"The mother nodded. She could hardly speak. The daughter burst into tears. I felt sure these people were hiding something.

" 'At what time did Mr. Drebber leave your house for the train?' I asked.

" 'At eight o'clock,' she said nervously. 'His secretary, Mr. Stangerson, said that there were two trains —one at 9:15 and one at 11. They wanted to catch the first one.'

" 'And was that the last time you saw him?'

"A terrible change came over the woman's face. It was some time before she could get out the single word 'Yes.' Her voice sounded strained.

"There was silence for a moment and then the daughter spoke in a calm, clear voice.

" 'No good ever came out of falsehood, mother,' she said. 'Let us be honest with this gentleman. We did see Mr. Drebber again.'

" 'God forgive you!' cried Madame Charpentier. She threw up her hands and sank back in her chair. 'You have murdered your brother.'

" 'Arthur would rather that we spoke the truth,' the girl answered firmly.

" 'You had best tell me all about it,' I said. 'You do not know how much Scotland Yard already knows.'

" 'It is on your head, Alice!' cried her mother. Then

she turned to me and said, 'I will tell you all, sir. My son is totally innocent. But I fear that you will think otherwise.'

" 'If your son is innocent he will come to no harm,' I commented.

" 'Perhaps, Alice, you had better leave us together,' she said. Her daughter withdrew. 'Now, sir,' she continued, 'Mr. Drebber has been with us three weeks. He and his secretary, Mr. Stangerson, had been traveling on the Continent. They had last been in Copenhagen. Stangerson was a quiet, reserved man. But Mr. Drebber was coarse and mean. He drank a good deal. He flirted with the maid servants. Worst of all he flirted with Alice—he once actually seized her and embraced her!'

" 'But why did you stand for this?' I asked. 'You should be able to get rid of your own boarders when you wish.'

"Mrs. Charpentier blushed. 'I should have turned him out immediately. But I am a poor widow and needed the money. My son is in the navy and has cost me much. But when Drebber grabbed my daughter I finally told him to leave. This was why he left. I didn't tell my son, who is on leave, anything of this. He has a violent temper and is very fond of his sister. I was glad to see Drebber and Stangerson go. Alas, an hour later there was a ring at the bell. It was Mr. Drebber. He was very excited and had been drinking again. He forced his way into the room where I was sitting with my daughter. He said that he had missed his train. Then he turned to Alice and asked her to fly off with him. "You are of age," he said. "There is no law to stop you. I have money enough. Never mind the old girl here. Come along with me. You shall live like a princess." Poor Alice was so frightened. She pulled away from him.

But he caught her wrist and pulled her toward the door. I screamed and at that moment my son Arthur came into the room. What happened then I do not know. I was too terrified to raise my head. I heard oaths and the sounds of a scuffle. When I did look up I saw Arthur standing in the doorway. He was laughing and held a stick in his hand. "I don't think that fine fellow will trouble us again," he said. "I will go after him and see what he does now." With those words he took his hat and started off down the street. The next morning we heard of Mr. Drebber's mysterious death.'

"This statement came from Mrs. Charpentier's own lips. At times she spoke so low that I could hardly catch the words. I made shorthand notes of all she said . . . so that there should be no possibility of a mistake."

"It's quite exciting," said Sherlock Holmes, with a yawn. "What happened next?"

"I asked her what time her son returned.

" 'I do not know,' she answered.

" 'Not know?'

" 'No. He has his own key. He let himself in.'

" 'After you went to bed?'

" 'Yes.'

" 'When did you go to bed?'

" 'About eleven.'

" 'So your son was gone at least two hours?'

" 'Yes.'

" 'What was he doing during that time?'

" 'I do not know,' she answered, and turned white to her very lips.

"Of course after that there was nothing more to be done. I found out where Lieutenant Charpentier was, took two officers with me and arrested him. When we arrested him, he said, 'I suppose you are arresting me for being concerned in the death of that scoundrel Drebber.' We had said nothing about it. His comment was thus very suspicious."

"Very," said Holmes.

"His mother had said he had carried a stick when he followed Drebber. He was still holding it. It was a thick piece of oak."

"What is your theory then?" Sherlock asked.

"Well, my theory is that he followed Drebber to Brixton Road. There they began to quarrel again. Charpentier must have struck him—perhaps in the stomach, which would leave no marks. The night was wet and there was no one about. Charpentier dragged him into the empty house. As to the candle, and the blood, and the writing on the wall, and the ring, they may all be so many tricks to throw the police off the scent."

"Well done!" said Holmes. "Really Gregson, you are doing well. We shall make a detective of you after all."

"I flatter myself that I have managed it rather neatly," the detective answered proudly. "The young man said that he had followed Drebber. Drebber saw that he was being followed and escaped him in a cab. On his way home, Charpentier met an old shipmate. They took a long walk together. I asked him where the shipmate lived, but he could not answer me. Obviously, he was telling me lies. I think the whole case fits together very well. What amuses me is that Lestrade is off on the wrong track. Why, by Jove, here's the very man himself!"

It was indeed Lestrade who now entered the room. He looked troubled and his clothes were untidy. On seeing his rival, he stood in the center of the room, not knowing quite what to do. "This is a most extraordinary case," he said at last.

"Ah, you find it so, Mr. Lestrade!" cried Gregson triumphantly. "I thought you would come to that conclusion. Have you managed to find the secretary, Mr. Joseph Stangerson?"

"The secretary, Mr. Joseph Stangerson," said Lestrade gravely, "was murdered at Halliday's Private Hotel at about six o'clock this morning."

Chapter 7
Light in the Darkness

We were dumbfounded at this news. Gregson sprang out of his chair and spilt his whiskey and water. I stared in silence at Sherlock. His lips were tight and his brows were drawn over his eyes.

"Stangerson, too!" he muttered. "The plot thickens."

"It was quite thick before," grumbled Lestrade. "I seem to have dropped into a sort of council of war."

"Are you—are you sure of this fact?" stammered Gregson.

"I have just come from his room," said Lestrade. "I was the first to discover what had occurred."

"We have been hearing Gregson's view of the matter," Holmes said. "Would you mind letting us know what you have seen and done?"

"Not at all," Lestrade answered. "I must admit that I believed Stangerson was involved in Drebber's death. I now see that I was mistaken. But believing I was correct, I set out to find Stangerson. Drebber and Stangerson had last been seen together at the train station. It was 8:30 P.M. on the evening of the 3rd. At two in the morning Drebber was found dead on Brixton Road. The questions now were: What had Stangerson done between 8:30 and the time of the crime and where was he now? First I telegraphed Liverpool and gave them a description of him. I asked them to keep watch for such a man who might board one of their boats to America. Next I started calling all the hotels and boarding houses near the train station. I figured that Drebber and Stangerson must have arranged a meeting place in case they were separated. At eight o'clock this morning I found Halliday's Private Hotel. Mr. Stangerson was staying there.

" 'No doubt you are the gentleman he is expecting,' they said. 'He has been waiting for a gentleman for two days.'

" 'Where is he now?' I asked.

" 'He is upstairs in bed. He wished to be called at nine.'

" 'I will go up and see him at once,' I said.

"The manager took me up to the room on the second floor. There was a small corridor leading to it. The manager pointed to the door and started down the stairs. Suddenly I saw something that made me feel sick—in spite of twenty years on the police force. There was a ribbon of blood coming from under the door! It had trickled out and formed a small pool in the hall. I gave a cry. The manager came back and nearly fainted on seeing it. The door was locked from the inside, but we put our shoulders to it and knocked it in. The window of the room was open. Huddled on the floor lay a dead man. His limbs were rigid and cold. When we turned him over the manager said that he was indeed Joseph Stangerson. The cause of death was a deep stab wound near the heart. And now comes the strangest part of the affair. What do you suppose was above the murdered man?"

I suddenly felt my flesh creep, even before he answered.

"The word RACHE written in letters of blood," said Sherlock Holmes.

"That was it," said Lestrade in a surprised voice. We were all silent for some time.

"The man was seen," continued Lestrade. "A delivery boy was walking down the lane early in the morning. He noticed a ladder leaning against a second floor window. He looked back and saw a man climbing down it. He says the man was tall, had a reddish face, and was dressed in a long, brownish coat. He must have stayed in Stangerson's room for some time after the murder. We found blood stains in the basin where he washed his hands. And there were blood marks on the sheets where he had wiped off his knife."

I glanced at Holmes. He had been correct in his description of the villain. The man was tall and flushed as Sherlock had deduced.

"Did you find clues in the room?" he asked.

"Nothing. Stangerson had Drebber's wallet in his pocket. That was not unusual as he was his secretary and paid all his bills. No money had been taken out. Robbery was certainly not the reason for these two crimes. There were no papers in the murdered man's pockets except a single telegram. It was a month old and came from Cleveland. It said 'J.H. IS IN EUROPE.' There was no signature."

"And there was nothing else?" Holmes asked.

"Nothing of importance. A book and a pipe were beside the bed. There was a glass of water on the table. On the windowsill was a small box containing a couple of pills."

Sherlock Holmes sprang out of his chair with an exclamation of delight.

"The last link!" he cried. "My case is complete."

The two detectives stared at him in amazement.

"I am now certain of all the main facts of the case—from the time Drebber left Stangerson at the station until the time of your discovery of Stangerson's body. I will give you a proof of my knowledge. Can you lay your hands on those pills?"

"I have them here," said Lestrade. He pulled out a small white box. "I was taking them, the purse, and the telegram to the police station for safekeeping. But I don't see anything important about the pills."

"Give them here," said Holmes. "Now, Doctor," turning to me, "are these ordinary pills?"

They certainly were not. They were of a pearly gray color and were small, round and almost clear. "From their color and lightness I believe they dissolve in water," I said.

"Precisely so," answered Holmes. "Now would you mind going down and fetching Mrs. Hudson's poor sickly terrier. She was asking you to put him out of his pain only yesterday."

I went downstairs and carried the dog upstairs in my arms. Its slow breathing and glassy eyes showed that it was already on death's door. I placed in on a cushion.

"I will now cut one of these pills in two," said Holmes. He pulled a penknife from his pocket and cut the pill. "One half we return to the pill box for another time. The other half I place in this glass with one teaspoon of water. You perceive that our friend, the doctor, was right. It quickly dissolves."

"This may be very interesting," said Lestrade. "But what does this have to do with the death of Mr. Joseph Stangerson?"

"Patience, my friend, patience! It has everything to do with it. I shall now add a little milk to make the mixture taste better. See how the dog laps it up."

Sherlock had poured the liquid into a saucer. The dog quickly licked it dry. We all watched the dog and waited for something to happen. But nothing did. The dog continued to lie stretched out on the cushion. The liquid seemed to have no effect.

Holmes looked particularly upset. He looked at his watch, chewed his lip, and drummed his fingers on the table. Both police detectives looked particularly pleased with his failure.

"It can't be a coincidence," he cried. Sherlock sprang from his chair and began to pace wildly up and down the room. "Surely my whole chain of reasoning cannot be incorrect. It is impossible! And yet this dog is still alive. Ah, I have it! I have it!" Sherlock rushed to the pillbox, and cut the other pill in two. He dissolved it in water, added milk, and gave it to the terrier. In a moment the dog was dead.

"I should have had more faith in my reasoning. Usually when something in a case does not fit, it is because you haven't thought about it from every angle. I now realize that one of the pills was harmless. The other was made of the most deadly poison. All this seems strange to you," he continued, "because you missed the one real clue in the case . . ."

"Look here, Mr. Sherlock Holmes," said Gregson, "we know you are a smart man and you have your own methods of working. It seems I was wrong about the case. Young Charpentier could not have been involved in Stangerson's death. He was in prison at the time. Lestrade thought Stangerson was the murderer, but that was wrong as well. Can you name the man who did it?"

"Yes. But his name is not important. What is important is to capture him. This I expect to do shortly. He is a clever and desperate man. I must be very careful catching him. One false move on my part and he will change his name and vanish in an instant. This is why I have not asked for your help. As soon as I can tell you, I shall."

Neither Lestrade nor Gregson seemed pleased with Mr. Sherlock Holmes' reply. But before they could speak there was a tap at the door. It was young Wiggins, the ringleader of Holmes' streetgang.

"Please, sir," he said, "I have the cab downstairs."

"Good boy," said Holmes. He turned to the two detectives. "Why don't you introduce these handcuffs at Scotland Yard?" he asked, taking a pair from his drawer. "See how beautifully the spring works. They fasten in an instant."

"The old type are good enough," answered Lestrade, "if we can only find the man to put them on."

"Very good, very good," said Holmes, smiling. Then he said to Wiggins: "The cabman may as well help me with my luggage. Just ask him to come up, Wiggins."

I was surprised to hear Sherlock speak of his luggage. He hadn't said anything to me about going on a journey. There was a small suitcase in the room. He now pulled it out and put it on the table. The cabman appeared just as Sherlock was strapping it closed.

"Just give me a hand with this buckle, cabman," he said.

The fellow reached toward the suitcase to fasten it. There was a sharp click. Sherlock had handcuffed the man.

"Gentlemen," he cried, "let me introduce you to Mr. Jefferson Hope, the murderer of Enoch Drebber and Joseph Stangerson."

For a moment we were all silent. Then suddenly the prisoner wrenched himself free of Holmes' grasp. He lunged toward the window. Glass and wood shattered before him. Lestrade, Gregson, and Holmes sprang upon him like bloodhounds and dragged him back into the room. A fierce struggle began. He was so strong that it took all four of us to hold him. We had to tie both his hands and feet to stop him from struggling.

"We have his cab," said Holmes, breathlessly. "It will serve to take him to Scotland Yard. And now, gentlemen, we have reached the end of our little mystery. I will be glad to answer your questions."

Part Two
The Country of the Saints

Chapter 1
On the Great Plain

There exists a great plain in the central portion of North America. It is bordered by the Sierra Mountains, looming high above it. The flat plain is a forbidding place, where few can survive for long. In winter the land is white with snow. In summer it is gray with dust. The coyote searches for food among the dry brush, the buzzard flaps heavily in the air, and the clumsy grizzly bear lumbers through the dark ravines and finds its food among the rocks. These are the plain's only inhabitants.

On the 4th of May, eighteen hundred and forty-seven, a lone traveler walked across the plain. His face was lean and haggard, his long, brown beard was flecked with gray. The man was dying—dying from hunger and from thirst. He climbed to a high point and looked over the plain for some sign of water. North, east, and west he looked. The great plain stretched before his eyes. There were no plants, no trees, no river in sight. Tired, he dropped his gray bundle on the ground and sat down. A little, moaning cry came from his parcel. A small, scared face with very bright brown eyes appeared.

"You've hurt me!" said a childish voice.

"Have I? I didn't mean to," answered the man. As he spoke he unwrapped the gray shawl and revealed a pretty little girl of about five years of age.

"How are you now?" he asked her.

"You bumped my head. Kiss it and make it well," she said. "That's what Mother used to do. Where's Mother?"

"Mother's gone. I guess you will see her before too long."

"Gone?" said the little girl. "Funny, she didn't say goodbye. She most always did if she was just going over to Auntie's for tea, and now she's been away three days. Say, it's awful dry here, isn't it? Isn't there any water or something to eat?"

"No, there's nothing, dearie. You remember when we left the river?"

"Oh, yes."

"Well, we reckoned we'd find another river soon. But something went wrong and we didn't. Our water ran out. Except for a little drop for you . . ."

"And you couldn't wash yourself," interrupted the girl, staring at the man's grimy face.

"No, nor drink. And Mr. Bender, he was the first to go, and then Indian Pete, and then Mrs. McGregor, and then Johnny Hones and then, dearie, your mother."

"Then Mother's dead, too," cried the little girl. She dropped her face and sobbed bitterly.

"Yes, they all died except you and me. So I heaved you onto my shoulder and started off in this direction. I thought we'd find water. But I was wrong. There's little chance for us now."

"Do you mean we are going to die too?" asked the girl.

"I guess that's about the size of it."

"Why didn't you say so before?" she said, laughing. "You gave me such a fright! Why, of course, as long as we die we'll be with Mother again."

"Yes, you will, dearie," the man said.

"And you, too. I'll tell her how awful good you've been. I'll bet she meets us at the door of heaven with a big pitcher of water and a lot of buckwheat cakes, hot and toasted on both sides like my brother Bob and me was fond of. How long will it be until we see her?"

"Not very long," answered the man. Above, three buzzards flew. The girl leaned on the man's chest and soon fell asleep. He watched over her for a long time, but he hadn't slept in three days. It was not long before he, too, was fast asleep.

Strangely enough, at that very moment their salvation was in sight. In the distance there rose up a great spray of dust. Canvas-covered wagons and horsemen were traveling across the plain. Thousands and thousands of them. It was a great caravan traveling west.

At the head of the caravan rode a group of plainly dressed, serious-looking men. They stopped to speak among themselves. One pointed to a tall mountain far in the distance. "To the right of the Sierra Blanca," he said, "so shall we reach the Rio Grande."

"Fear not for water," cried another, "God will not abandon His own chosen people."

"Amen! Amen!" responded the whole party.

Just then one of the younger men cried out. He

pointed to a crag above them. A wisp of pink cloth fluttered against the rocks. The men reined in their horses and took out their guns. The word "Redskins" was on their lips.

"There can't be any Indians here," said the leader. "We have passed the Pawnees and there are no other tribes until we cross the great mountains."

"Shall I go forward and see, Brother Stangerson?" asked one of the band.

"And I," "and I," cried a dozen voices.

"Leave your horses below and we will await you here," the elder answered. In a moment the young men had dismounted and were climbing up the slope. Soon there was a cry of astonishment from above. They had come upon the man and the little girl.

The cry awoke the two sleepers. They stared about them in bewilderment. The man staggered to his feet. He looked down onto the plain. It had been empty before he went to sleep. Now, it was teeming with life. He could hardly believe his eyes.

The rescuing party quickly convinced him this was no dream. One of them lifted the child onto his shoulders. Two others helped the weakened man walk toward the wagons.

"My name is John Ferrier," the man explained. "Me and the little one are all that is left of twenty-one people. The rest are all dead of thirst and hunger."

"Is she your child?" someone asked.

"I guess she is now," the man said strongly. "She's mine 'cause I saved her. No man will take her from me. She's Lucy Ferrier from this day on. Who are you?" he asked. "There seems to be a powerful lot of you."

"Near ten thousand," said one of the young men. "We are children of God. We are the Mormons."

John Ferrier had heard of the Mormons. They were a religious group.

"And where are you going?" he asked.

"We do not know. The hand of God is leading us through our Prophet, Brigham Young. You must come before him. He shall say what is to be done with you."

The men took John and Lucy Ferrier past pale-faced women, strong, laughing children, and anxious men. They all exclaimed on seeing the strange pair. They were taken to a huge wagon. Sitting next to the driver was a young man. He was reading a brown-backed volume. He laid the book aside and listened to his men. Then he turned to the foundlings.

"If we take you with us," he said in solemn words, "it can only be as believers in our religion. We must all be united by our faith. Will you come with us on these terms?"

"Guess I'll come with you on any terms," said Ferrier.

"Take him, Brother Stangerson," the leader said. "Give him and the child food and drink. Let it be your task to teach him our beliefs. We have delayed enough. Forward!"

With a crackling of whips and the creaking of wheels the great caravan began to move once more. Brother Stangerson took the man and the girl to his wagon. A meal was already waiting.

"You shall remain here," Brother Stangerson said. "In a few days you will be stronger. In the meantime remember that now and forever you are of our religion. Brigham Young has said it."

Chapter 2
The Flower of Utah

The great caravan traveled on until it reached the broad valley of Utah. There the Mormons settled. It was not long before they were farming the land and building a great city which they called Salt Lake City. Lucy and her father traveled with them to their new land. By journey's end, Lucy was a pet with the women, and John was respected by all. It was agreed that he should receive as large and fertile a piece of land as any—with the exception of Brigham Young and the Council of Four. The Council of Four was made up of Elders Stangerson, Kemball, Johnston, and Drebber. They presided over the people, and so were entitled to larger homesteads.

John built himself a large log house. Over the years he added to it until it became a roomy villa. He worked his farm morning and night. In three years he was better off than his neighbors. In six he was well-to-do. In nine he was rich. And in twelve there were few men in all Salt Lake City who could compare with him. By then his name was known far and wide.

There was only one way in which John Ferrier went against his new religion. The Mormons of that time believed in marrying many wives. But John Ferrier did not marry. In all other ways he took on the habits of his new faith.

Lucy Ferrier grew up in the log house and helped her stepfather with his work. Each year she grew taller and stronger. She was so pretty that many considered her the loveliest flower in all Utah.

One warm June morning, Lucy rode her horse to town. She had a task to perform for her father. Near town, she found the road blocked by a great herd of cattle. She tried to pass them by pushing her horse into a small gap. But the cattle closed in behind her. She urged her horse on but the horns of a bull prodded him. He became excited and began to prance and toss. Every plunge of the horse pushed him against the bull's horns. The situation worsened. Lucy's head began to swim. Her grip began to loosen. Suddenly she heard a voice at her side. A strong, tanned hand took hold of her horse's reins and led her to safety.

"You're not hurt, I hope, miss," said her rescuer.

She looked up at the young man's face and laughed. "I'm awful frightened," she said. "Who'd have thought my horse, Poncho, would be so scared of a lot of cows."

"Thank God, you kept your seat," the young man said. "I guess you are the daughter of John Ferrier," he remarked. "I saw you ride down from his house. When you see him, ask him if he remembers the Jefferson Hopes of St. Louis. If he's the same Ferrier, my father and he were friends."

"Why don't you come and ask him yourself?"

The young fellow seemed pleased at the suggestion. "I'll do so," he said. "We've been hunting in the mountains for two months. I'm not exactly presentable. He'll have to take me as he finds me."

"He has a good deal to thank you for, and so have I," she answered. "He's awful fond of me. If those cows had jumped on me he'd have never got over it."

"Neither would I," said her companion.

"You? Well, I don't see that it would make much difference to you. You're not even a friend of ours."

The young hunter's face grew so gloomy over her remark that Lucy Ferrier laughed aloud.

"There, I didn't mean that," she said. "Of course you are a friend now. You must come and see us. Now I must push along or Father won't trust me with his business anymore. Goodbye!"

"Goodbye," he answered, raising his sombrero. She turned her horse around, gave a crack to her whip, and was off down the broad road in a cloud of dust.

Young Jefferson Hope rode on, but his mind was on Lucy Ferrier. Their short meeting had stirred something in his heart. He knew he would never be the same again. He swore to himself that he would win her love.

He called on John Ferrier that night and many times again. Soon his face was a familiar one at the farmhouse. John had spent these last twelve years cooped up in the valley. He had had little chance to learn about the outside world. Jefferson Hope was able to tell him all he wanted to know. He had been a pioneer in California. He had been a scout and a trapper and a silver explorer and a ranchman. He had had many adventures and could tell a story better than most. He soon became a favorite with the old farmer. When he visited, Lucy was silent . . . but her blushing cheeks and bright happy eyes showed that she had lost her heart. Her father may not have noticed that his daughter was in love, but Jefferson Hope did.

One evening he came galloping down the road and pulled up at their gate. Lucy came down to meet him. He threw the bridle over the fence and jumped off his horse.

"I am off, Lucy," he said. He took her two hands in his. "I won't ask you to come with me now. But will you be ready to come when I am here again?"

"And when will that be?" she asked, blushing and laughing.

"In a couple of months. I will come and marry you then, my darling. There's no one who can stand between us."

"And how about Father?" she asked.

"He has given his consent."

"Of course, if you and Father have arranged it all, there's no more to be said," she whispered.

"Thank God!" he said. "It is settled then. The longer I stay, the harder it will be to go. Goodbye, my own darling, goodbye. In two months you shall see me."

He got up onto his horse and rode away from her without looking back. Lucy stood at the gate and gazed after him until he had vanished from her sight. Then she walked back into the house. She was the happiest girl in Utah.

Chapter 3
John Ferrier Talks
with the Prophet

Three weeks had passed since Jefferson Hope left Salt Lake City. John Ferrier was sad to think his daughter would soon leave him. But her bright and happy face told him that it was the right thing. Long ago he had decided that she should never marry a Mormon. He could never accept polygamy—the marrying of more than one wife to one man. To him it was shameful and a disgrace. But he never told anyone his feelings. He was afraid harm would come to him and his lovely daughter.

Yes, in those days it was a dangerous matter to disagree with the Mormon faith. There existed a secret band of Mormon men called the Avenging Angels. The Avenging Angels took it upon themselves to enforce the laws of the Mormon faith—however violently. It was not uncommon for men to simply disappear without a trace, never to be seen again. Their wives and children would wait for them to come home night after night, but they never did. Neighbor began to fear neighbor, each afraid to speak of his or her beliefs. Each afraid that the other belonged to the secret band.

One fine morning John Ferrier looked out his window. He saw a stout, sandy-haired man come up the pathway. His heart leaped into his mouth. It was none other than the great Brigham Young himself. Full of fear, Ferrier ran to the door to meet the Mormon chief. Young walked into the sitting room.

"Brother Ferrier," he said, taking a seat. "We Mormons have been good friends to you. We picked you up when you were starving on the plain. We shared our food with you. We led you to safety in this valley. We gave you a good share of land and allowed you to become rich. Is this not so?"

"It is so," answered John Ferrier.

"In return for all this we asked but one thing—that

you embrace our faith. This you promised to do, but you have not done so."

"Have I not given money to the church?" John Ferrier asked. "Have I not attended the Temple? Have I not—?"

"Where are your wives?" asked Young. "Call them in, that I may greet them."

"It is true that I have not married," Ferrier answered. "But women were few and there were many who had better claims than I. I was not a lonely man. I had my daughter to attend to my wants."

"It is of your daughter that I would speak to you," said the leader of the Mormons. "She has grown to be the flower of Utah. She has found favor in the eyes of many."

John Ferrier groaned silently.

"There are stories that I would prefer not to believe . . . stories that she is engaged to some Gentile. This must be the gossip of idle tongues. You know only too well our rule that each Mormon girl must marry a Mormon man. To marry a Gentile is a crime against the church."

John Ferrier made no answer.

"Your whole faith shall be tested upon this one point. The girl is young. We would not have her wed gray hairs. Nor would we deprive her of all choice. We Elders already have many wives, but our children must also be provided for. Stangerson has a son, and Drebber has a son. Either of them would gladly welcome your daughter to his house. Let her choose between them. They are young and rich and of the true faith. What say you to that?"

Ferrier remained silent for some time with his brows knit.

"You will give us time," he said at last. "My daughter is very young. She is scarce of an age to marry."

"She shall have one month to choose," said Young. He rose from his seat. "At the end of that time she shall give her answer."

As Young went to leave, he turned and said sternly, "It would be better for you and her to be skeletons on the plain than to go against the Council of Four."

John Ferrier sat wondering how to speak of this matter with his dear daughter. Suddenly a soft hand touched his. She was standing beside him. Her pale, frightened face told him that she had heard all.

"I could not help it," she said. "His voice rang through the house. Oh Father, Father, what shall we do?"

"Don't scare yourself," he answered. "We'll fix it up somehow or other. You haven't stopped caring for Jefferson, have you?"

A sob and a squeeze of the hand were her only answer.

"No, of course not. I shouldn't care to hear you say you did. He's a good lad and he's a Christian . . . which is more than these folks here—in spite of their praying and preaching. I have a friend leaving for Nevada tomorrow. I'll send Jefferson a message letting him know the hole we are in. If I know anything of that young man, he'll be back with a speed that would whip electro-telegraph."

Lucy laughed through her tears.

"When he comes, he will advise us for the best," she said. "But it is for you that I am frightened, dear. One hears—one hears such dreadful stories about those who oppose the Prophet. Something terrible always happens to them."

"But we haven't opposed him yet," her father answered. "We have a clear month before us. At the end of that I guess we'll leave Utah."

"Leave Utah!"

"That's about the size of it."

"But the farm?"

"We will raise as much money as we can and let the rest go. To tell the truth this isn't the first time I have thought of going. I don't like bowing down to any man, like these folks do to their darned Prophet. I'm a free-born American. If he comes looking around this farm again, he just might run up against some buckshot."

"But they won't let us leave," his daughter said.

"Wait 'til Jefferson comes. We'll manage it. In the meantime, don't you fret yourself, my dearie. And don't go crying and swelling up your pretty eyes. There's nothing to be afraid of and there's no danger at all."

John Ferrier said these words in a very confident tone. But that night, Lucy noticed her father cleaned and loaded his old shotgun. And from then on he bolted the farmdoors shut.

Chapter 4
A Flight for Life

The next morning John Ferrier went to town. He found his friend and gave him a message for Jefferson Hope. The message told of Young's visit and that they had been given a month to decide who Lucy would marry. It begged him to return at once. Ferrier returned home feeling much better.

He was surprised to find two horses hitched to the gateposts. He found two young men lounging in his sitting room. One had a long pale face. He was leaning back in the rocking chair with his feet against the stove. The other had a thick neck and coarse features. He was standing in front of the windows with his hands in his pockets. Both nodded to Ferrier as he entered. The one in the rocking chair was the first to speak.

"Maybe you don't know us," he said. "This here is the son of Elder Drebber, and I'm Joseph Stangerson. I traveled with you in my father's wagon across the plain."

John Ferrier bowed coldly. He had guessed who his visitors were.

"We have come," continued Stangerson, "at the advice of our fathers. Your daughter is to choose between us. I have but four wives and Brother Drebber here has seven. It appears to me that my claim is the stronger one."

"Nay, nay, Brother Stangerson," cried the other. "The question is not how many wives we have. It is how many we can afford. My father has given me his mills. I am the richer man."

"When my father dies I shall have his tanning yard and his leather factory. Also, I am older than you and higher in the Church," Stangerson said.

"It will be for the maiden to decide," said young Drebber. "We will leave it all to her decision."

John Ferrier stood at the door fuming. He was hardly able to keep his riding whip off his two visitors' backs.

"Look here," he said at last. "When my daughter

summons you, you can come. Until then I don't want to see your faces again."

The two young Mormons stared at him in amazement.

"There are two ways out of the room," cried Ferrier. "There is the door, and there is the window. Which do you care to use?"

His brown face looked so savage, and his thin hands so threatening, that his visitors sprang to their feet and rushed to the door.

"You shall suffer for this!" Stangerson said. "You have gone against the Prophet and the Council of Four. You shall live to regret it."

"The hand of the Lord will be heavy on you," cried young Drebber. "He will strike you!"

"Then I'll start striking!" exclaimed Ferrier. He was just about to rush upstairs and fetch his gun when Lucy seized his arm. Meanwhile, the clatter of horses' hoofs told them the young men had fled.

"The young rascals!" Ferrier exclaimed. "I would sooner see you in your grave than married to either of them."

"And so should I, Father," she answered. "But Jefferson will soon be here."

"Yes. It will not be long before he comes. The sooner the better. We don't know what their next move will be."

Ferrier knew that his wealth and position would not help him now. No one had ever gone against the Prophet in such a way. If others were punished so harshly for lesser crimes, then what would be his fate? He was a brave man, but he trembled at the vague, shadowy terrors that hung over him. He hid his fears from his daughter and tried to make light of it. But she knew he was deeply worried.

Ferrier knew he would hear from Young. He was not mistaken. On rising the next morning he found a note. It was pinned to his quilt, just above his chest. On it was printed in bold letters:

YOU HAVE TWENTY-NINE DAYS
TO REPENT AND THEN—

How did the note come into his room? The doors and windows were locked. The servants slept in an outhouse. He crumbled the paper up and said nothing to his daughter. But he was afraid. How could one fight an enemy with such mysterious powers? The hand which fastened that pin to his quilt could have struck him in the heart. He would never have known who had slain him.

He was even more shaken the next morning. They had sat down to breakfast. Lucy gave a cry of surprise and pointed upward. In the center of the ceiling was scrawled the number 28. Lucy did not understand, but Ferrier knew only too well what it meant. Brigham Young had given him one month to agree to Lucy marrying one of the Elders' sons. At the end of that month something terrible would happen. Of that he was sure. The numbers represented the days left until that month was up. That night he sat up with his gun and kept watch. He saw and he heard nothing. Yet in the morning a great 27 was painted on the outside of his door.

And so it went each day. Every morning he found the numbers written in some obvious place. Sometimes the fatal numbers appeared upon the walls, sometimes upon the floors, sometimes on the garden gate or railings. Ferrier never saw the men who wrote it, but he knew they were the Avenging Angels. And he knew at the end of the month it would be they who would harm him and his daughter. As the month passed he became worn and restless. His eyes took on the troubled look of a hunted animal. He had only one hope in life now. And that was for Jefferson Hope to arrive in time.

One by one the numbers dwindled down and still no sign of Jefferson Hope. When five gave way to four and four to three, John Ferrier gave up hope. He did not know what terrible thing awaited him, but he knew he could not escape. He did not know the surrounding mountains well enough to travel them at night. The roads were guarded . . . no one could pass without an order from the Council. No, no one had ever refused Young's orders before. The Avenging Angels would make him pay. Still, the old man stood firm. He would rather die than see his daughter married to young Drebber or Stangerson.

Finally the end of the month came. Ferrier was sitting alone, searching in his mind for some way out. That morning he had found a 2 on the wall of his house. The next day would be the last. What was to happen then? Terrible thoughts filled his imagination. And his daughter? What would happen to her after he was gone?

What was that? In the silence he heard a gentle scratching sound. It came from the door of the house. Ferrier crept into the hall to listen. Someone was definitely tapping on the door. Was it an assassin come to murder him in the night? Or was it someone writing the number 1 upon his door? John Ferrier could not stand the suspense. He sprang forward, drew the bolt and threw the door open.

Outside all was calm and quiet. The night was fine and the stars were twinkling. There was no sign of any human being. Ferrier looked to the right, and then to the left—no one. Then he glanced down. To his astonishment he saw a man lying flat on his face.

At first he thought the man was dead but then he saw the figure begin to crawl. It crawled along the ground and into the hall as quickly and noiselessly as a snake. Once in the house, the man sprang to his feet, and closed the door. It was none other than Jefferson Hope.

"Good God!" gasped John Ferrier. "How you scared me! Whatever made you come in like that?"

"Give me food," said Hope. "I have had no time for food or drink in forty-eight hours." There was still some supper on the table. This he started to devour. "How is Lucy?" he asked, when he had satisfied his hunger.

"She does not know the danger," her father answered.

"That is well," said Hope. "The house is watched on every side. That is why I crawled my way up to it. They may be darned sharp, but they're not sharp enough to catch a hunter like me."

John Ferrier grabbed the young man's hand and shook it. "You're a man to be proud of. There are not many who would come to share our danger and our troubles."

"It's true," the young hunter answered. "I have respect for you, but if you were alone I might think twice before I stuck my head into this hornet's nest. It's Lucy that brings me here. Before any harm comes to her I guess there will be one less of the Hope family in Utah."

"What are we to do?" Ferrier asked.

"Tomorrow is your last day. You must act tonight or be lost. I have a mule and two horses waiting in the Eagle Ravine. How much money have you?"

"Two thousand dollars in gold, and five in notes."

"That will do. I have as much to add. We must push for Carson City through the mountains. You had best wake Lucy. It is well the servants do not sleep in the house."

Ferrier went to wake Lucy and prepare her for the journey. Meanwhile Jefferson Hope made a parcel of food and filled a stoneware jar with water. Soon Ferrier returned with his daughter. The lovers greeted each other warmly, but briefly. There was no time to lose.

"We must make our start at once," said Hope. "The front and back entrances are watched. With caution we can escape through the side window and across the fields. Once on the road it is only two miles to the Eagle Ravine where the horses are waiting. By daybreak we should be halfway through the mountains."

"What if we are stopped?" asked Ferrier.

Hope slapped his revolver. "If they are too many for us, we'll take two or three with us to the grave," he said with a sinister smile.

They turned out the lights of the house. Ferrier carried the bag of gold and notes. Lucy had a small bundle with her most valued possessions. And Hope had the food and water. They opened the window slowly and carefully. When a dark cloud passed over, making the night dark, they climbed out. They held their breath and crouched down, then they scrambled through the garden. They were just about to run into the cornfield beyond, when Hope dragged them behind a hedge.

Suddenly there came the sound of a mountain owl a few yards from them. This was answered by another hoot some distance away. Then there appeared a man who repeated the signal. With that the second man rose up.

"Tomorrow at midnight," said the first. "When the owl calls three times."

"It is well," said the other. "Shall I tell Brother Drebber?"

"Pass it on to him. And from him to others. Nine to seven!"

"Seven to five!" said the other. The two figures flitted away in different directions. Their last words were obviously some form of signal. The instant their footsteps died away, Jefferson Hope sprang to his feet, and led the way across the fields at top speed.

"Hurry on, hurry on!" he gasped from time to time. "We are through the line of sentries. Everything depends on speed. Hurry on!"

They made rapid progress once they were on the road. Before reaching town, they took a rugged and narrow footpath into the mountains. Two dark jagged peaks loomed above them. It was not long before they reached the animals. Lucy was placed on the mule, old Ferrier on one of the horses, and Jefferson on the other. Jefferson was a skilled scout and hunter and he led them through the rugged mountains. Despite their danger, each of the party felt lighthearted. Each step led them closer and closer to freedom.

They had reached the wildest portion of the pass

when the girl gave a startled cry. She pointed upward. On a rock overlooking their path, stood a man with a rifle. His call, "Who goes there?" rang out through the night.

"Travelers from Nevada," said Jefferson Hope. He placed one hand on his rifle.

"By whose permission?" cried the sentry.

"The Council of Four," answered Ferrier.

"Nine to seven," cried the sentry.

"Seven to five," called Jefferson promptly, remembering the signal he had heard in the garden.

"Pass, and the Lord go with you," said the voice from above. Soon the path broadened and the horses were able to break into a trot. Looking back, they could see the lone guard leaning upon his gun. They had passed Mormon territory. Freedom lay ahead.

Chapter 5
The Avenging Angels

All night they traveled through dangerous mountain passes. They finally stopped at a mountain stream to water their horses and have breakfast. Lucy and her father wanted to rest longer, but Jefferson Hope was firm. "They will be on our track by this time," he said. "Everything depends on our speed. Once safe in Carson, we may rest for the remainder of our lives."

They continued through the mountains all day. By evening they figured they were more than thirty miles from their enemies. At night they rested at the base of a rocky crag and huddled together for warmth. By daybreak they were up and on their way once more. They had seen nothing of their pursuers and Hope was beginning to think that they were now out of their reach.

About the middle of the second day their provisions began to run out. Being a good hunter, Hope was not worried. He made a fire where Lucy and her father could warm themselves and said goodbye to Lucy. Then he slung his gun over his shoulder and set off in search of food. Looking back, he saw the old man and the young girl crouching over the blazing fire. The three animals stood motionless in the background.

He walked for some time without finding any game. After two or three hours he decided to turn back. Just then, he saw a bighorn sheep. He rested his rifle on a rock, took aim, and drew the trigger. The animal sprang into the air, tottered for a moment and then fell to the ground.

The creature was too large to carry, so Jefferson cut a haunch and flank. He put his trophy over his shoulder and hastened to retrace his steps. By now it was evening. Hope had gone far in his search for meat. The terrain no longer looked familiar. He lost his way many times. The meat was heavy and he stumbled along. But he kept on, for every step brought him closer to his Lucy. The meat he carried would enable them to finish their journey.

Finally Jefferson reached the area where he had left Lucy and her father. Their camp was only a short distance away. It was now five hours since he had left. They must be worried about him. He put his hands to his mouth and shouted a loud halloo. The mountains echoed with his voice. He paused and listened for an answer. None came.

Again he shouted, even louder than before. Again there was no answer. Dread filled his heart. He hurried on, dropping the precious food in his rush.

He could soon see the spot where the fire had been. There was still a glowing pile of wood ashes there. He rushed forward. No living creature was to be seen. Animals, man, maiden, all were gone. It was clear that a sudden and terrible disaster had occurred.

Hope was bewildered and stunned. He seized a smoldering piece of wood, and blew it into a flame. By its light, he started to examine the little camp. The ground was stamped down by the feet of many horses. A large party of men had overtaken the Ferriers. From the direction of their tracks he could see that they had afterwards returned to Salt Lake City. Had they carried back both of his companions? He had begun to think so when his eyes caught sight of something. It was a heap of reddish soil. Every nerve in his body began to tingle. There was no mistaking it for anything but a newly-dug grave. A twig was stuck in the earth. A piece of paper dangled from it. On the paper was written these words:

JOHN FERRIER
FORMERLY OF SALT LAKE CITY
died August 4th, 1860

So, the sturdy old man was dead. Jefferson Hope looked wildly around him for a second grave. There was none. Lucy must have been carried back to marry one of the Elders' sons. Right then and there Jefferson Hope pledged to get revenge. He would devote his life to that end. He retraced his steps to where he had dropped the meat. He stirred up the fire and cooked enough to last him a few days. He made up a bundle and tired as he was, set out on foot through the mountains to find the Avenging Angels.

Weary and footsore, he walked for five days. At night he flung himself onto the rocks and snatched a few hours sleep. By daybreak he was always on his way. On the sixth day he reached the Eagle Ravine where they had started their ill-fated flight. From there, he could see the city down below. Flags and banners were flying in the streets. Just as he was wondering what they could mean, a man rode toward him. It was a Mormon named Cowper. Hope recognized the man and stopped him in the hopes of finding out what Lucy Ferrier's fate had been.

"I am Jefferson Hope," he said. "You remember me?"

The Mormon looked at him in astonishment. This white-faced, fierce-eyed man hardly looked like that young strong hunter.

"You are mad to come here!" he cried. "It is dangerous for me to even speak with you. There is a warrant against you for helping the Ferriers escape."

"I don't fear them, or their warrant," Hope said. "You must know something of this matter, Cowper. I beg you to answer a few questions. For God's sake don't refuse me!"

"What is it?" the Mormon asked uneasily. "Be quick, the very rocks have ears and the trees eyes."

"What has become of Lucy Ferrier?"

"She was married yesterday to Young Drebber. Are you all right?"

Hope had nearly fainted. "Married you say?" he said feebly.

"Married yesterday—that's what those flags are for.

Young Drebber and Young Stangerson argued over who would have her. They'd both been in the search party. Stangerson had shot her father and so seemed to have the best claim. But the Council decided to give her to Drebber. No one will have her very long though. I saw death in her face yesterday. She is more like a ghost than a woman. Are you off then?"

"Yes, I am off," said Jefferson Hope, who had risen. His face was hard as marble and his eyes glowed with sadness and hate.

"Where are you going?"

"Never mind," he answered and strode off into the mountains.

The Mormon was right. Lucy Ferrier pined away and died within a month. Drebber cared more for her father's property than he did for her, and did not grieve. But his many wives mourned over her dead body in the Mormon tradition. The night before she was to be buried, a strange thing happened in Drebber's house. A savage-looking, weather-beaten man in tattered garments strode into Lucy's room. He walked straight up to the white body that had been hers. Stooping over her, he pressed his lips to her cold forehead. Then he snatched up her hand and took the wedding ring from her finger. "She shall not be buried in that," he cried with a fierce snarl. He was gone before an alarm could be raised.

For some months Jefferson Hope remained in the mountains. Sometimes he was seen prowling outside the city. Once a bullet whistled through Stangerson's window, within a foot of him. Another time, Drebber passed under a cliff when a boulder crashed down, nearly killing him.

The two young Mormons knew only too well who was making attempts on their lives. They searched for Hope in the mountains, but without success. They never went out alone and had their houses guarded. After a while they began to relax. Nothing had been seen of Jefferson Hope in some time. They believed his anger had cooled with time.

But time had heightened Jefferson Hope's anger. He knew he could not go on living in the mountains without food or money. And so he decided to work in the Nevada mines for a year. As it turned out, he could not leave for five years. But his craving for revenge had not lessened. Disguised, he returned to Salt Lake City. There he found that a group of Mormons had rebelled against the Elders. They had left Utah and become Gentiles. Drebber and Stangerson were in the group. No one knew where they had gone. It was said that Drebber had left a wealthy man while Stangerson was now poor.

Jefferson Hope did not give up. He was determined to have his revenge. He went from state to state looking for his enemies. Year passed into year and his hair turned gray. But he wandered on—a human bloodhound. At last his efforts were rewarded. In Cleveland, Ohio, he caught a glance of Drebber in a window. He returned to his miserable lodgings to make a plan. But it so happened that Drebber had seen him too—and seen murder in his eyes. He and Stangerson rushed to the justice of the peace. They complained that their lives were threatened by an old rival. That evening Jefferson Hope was arrested. By the time he was freed, both Drebber and Stangerson had departed for Europe.

Eventually Hope earned enough money to travel after them. He followed them from city to city, always missing them. At last he caught up with them in London. As to what happened there, we must return to Dr. Watson's journal.

Chapter 6
A Continuation of John Watson's Journal

Our prisoner calmed down when he saw that he was indeed captured. He even smiled and said he hoped that he hadn't hurt any of us in the scuffle. "I guess you're going to take me to the police station," he remarked to Sherlock Holmes. "My cab's at the door. If you untie my legs, I'll walk down to it. I'm not as light to lift as I used to be."

Gregson and Lestrade looked at each other nervously. They were afraid the prisoner would bolt. But Holmes took him at his word and untied his legs. The prisoner rose and stretched his legs. I had seldom seen a more powerfully built man.

"If there is a vacant place for chief of police," he told Holmes, "then I reckon you are the man for the job. The way you kept on my trail was admirable."

"We had better all go to the station," said Holmes.

"I can drive the cab," said Lestrade.

"Good! Gregson you can come inside with me. You, too, Doctor."

We all went down the stairs together. Our prisoner

made no attempt to escape. He stepped calmly into the cab and we followed him. Lestrade mounted the box, whipped up the horse and drove us quickly to the station. There, we were led into a small chamber. The prisoner's name was noted as were the names of the two men he had murdered. "The prisoner will be brought to trial in a week," the police inspector said. "In the meantime, Mr. Jefferson Hope, do you have anything to say? I must warn you that your words will be written down and may be used against you at your trial."

"I've got a great deal to say," our prisoner said slowly. "I want to tell you gentlemen all about it."

"Hadn't you better wait till your trial?" asked the Inspector.

"I may never be tried," he answered. "You needn't look so startled. I'm not thinking of suicide. Are you a doctor?" He turned his fierce eyes toward me.

"Yes, I am," I answered.

"Then put your hand here," he said. He motioned toward his chest.

I put my hand over his heart. His chest was throbbing unnaturally. In the silent room I could hear the loud and irregular beating of his heart. I knew immediately that the artery around the heart was abnormally swollen . . . an almost always fatal condition.

"I went to the doctor last week," Jefferson Hope said. "He told me that the artery was bound to burst within a few days. It has been getting worse for years. I got it from living in bad conditions in the Salt Lake Mountains. I've done my work now, and I don't care how soon I die. But I should like to leave some account of this business. I don't want to be remembered as a cutthroat."

Jefferson Hope leaned back in his chair and began the following remarkable statement.

"It doesn't matter to you why I hated these men," he said. "It's enough that they are guilty of the death of two human beings—a father and a daughter. Too much time had passed for them to be convicted of their crimes. But I knew of their guilt and decided to be their judge, jury, and executioner.

"Twenty years ago that girl was to marry me. She was forced instead to marry this same Drebber. She broke her heart over it. I took the marriage ring from her dead finger and I vowed that Drebber's dying eyes should look on it. His last thoughts should be of the terrible crime he had committed. I have carried it about with me and have followed him and his accomplice over two continents. They thought they could tire me out. But they could not do it. If I die tomorrow, I die knowing my work in this world is done—well done. They have died and by my hand. There is nothing left for me to hope for or desire.

"They were rich and I was poor. It was no easy matter for me to follow them. When I got to London my pocket was empty. I had to earn a living. I inquired and inquired until at last I found them. They were at a boarding house on the other side of the river. Once I found them, I knew they were at my mercy. I had grown my beard and I knew they would not recognize me. I would follow them until I found my chance. They would not escape me again.

"Sometimes I followed them in my cab, sometimes on foot. They were very clever though, and never traveled alone. At last my chance came. I was driving on their street when I saw a cab pull up to their door. Presently some luggage was brought out. After a time Stangerson and Drebber boarded the cab and it drove off. I whipped my horse and followed closely. They got off at the train station. I found a boy to look after my horse and cab and followed them onto the platform. I heard them ask the guard for the Liverpool train. He answered that one had just gone. There would not be another for some hours. Stangerson seemed upset at that but Drebber seemed rather pleased. He said he had an errand to run and would meet Stangerson on the platform in two hours. Stangerson argued that they should not be separated. But Drebber answered that he was nothing but his paid servant and could not tell him what to do. They agreed to meet at the Halliday's Private Hotel if Drebber missed the last train.

"The moment I had waited for had come. I had my enemies in my power. Together they could protect each other. Apart, they were at my mercy. It was important for each to know who was punishing them and why. I already had my plan. A few days before a man had been looking at some empty houses on Brixton Road. He dropped one of the keys in my cab. I had a copy made before it was claimed. I now had a place where I could take Drebber. The question now was—how do I get him there?

"Drebber left the station and I followed him. He went into several taverns. When he came out of the last, he was drunk. He hailed a cab. Again I followed. He went back to his boarding house. He entered it and his cab drove away. Give me a glass of water please. My mouth gets dry from talking."

I handed him a glass and he drank it down.

"That's better," he said. "Well, I waited a quarter of an hour or more. Suddenly there came a noise from inside the house . . . like people fighting. Next moment the door flung open. Two men appeared. One was Drebber and the other was a young man I had never seen before. This fellow had Drebber by the collar. He shoved and kicked Drebber down the stairs and into the road. 'You hound!' he cried and shook his stick at him. 'I'll teach you to insult an honest girl.' He was so mad I thought he was going to hit Drebber with his stick. But Drebber staggered away down the road as fast as his legs would carry him. He was at the corner when he saw my cab, hailed it, and jumped in. 'Drive me to Halliday's Private Hotel,' said he.

"I had him! My heart was fairly jumping for joy. I was afraid my artery would burst any moment! I drove slowly along wondering what to do next. He answered my problem for me. He ordered me to stop at a drinking place and wait for him. When he came out he was so drunk he could hardly see.

"I had no intention of killing him in cold blood. I had two pillboxes on me—one for Drebber and one for Stangerson. Each contained one poisoned pill and one harmless pill. I would let Drebber choose one pill from the box while I would eat the pill that remained. It would be up to fate who lived and who died.

"It was near one o'clock. It was a wild bleak night. The rain was coming down in torrents. I lit a cigar and puffed on it to steady my nerves. My hands shook with excitement.

"There was not a soul to be seen, nor a sound to be heard, except the dripping rain. When we reached Brixton

Road, I opened the cab door. Drebber was all huddled up in a drunken sleep. I shook his arm. 'It's time to get out,' I said.

" 'All right, cabby,' said he.

"I suppose he thought he had come to the hotel. He got out without another word and followed me down the garden. I had to walk beside him to keep him steady. I opened the door and led him into the front room.

" 'It's awfully dark,' he said.

" 'We'll soon have light,' I replied. I struck a match and lit a candle I had brought. 'Now Enoch Drebber,' I continued, 'Who am I?' I held the candle to my face.

"He gazed at me with drunken eyes. Then I saw horror spring up in them. He staggered back and broke into a sweat. His teeth began to chatter in his head. I just leaned against the door and laughed.

" 'You dog!' I said. 'I have hunted you from Salt Lake City to St. Petersburg. You have always escaped me. Now your wanderings have come to an end. One of us will never see tomorrow.' I could see on his face that he thought I was mad. And at that moment I was. I was so keyed up that my nose started to bleed.

" 'What do you think of Lucy Ferrier now?' I cried, locking the door and shaking the key in his face. 'Punishment has been slow in coming, but it has overtaken you at last.' His lips trembled as I spoke.

" 'Would you murder me?' he stammered.

" 'It is not murder to kill a mad dog. You had no mercy on my poor darling. You dragged her from her slaughtered father and took her to your shameless harem.'

" 'It was not I who killed her father,' he cried.

" 'But it was you who broke her innocent heart,' I shrieked. I thrust one of my pillboxes toward him. 'Let the high God judge between us. Choose and eat. There is death in one and life in the other. I shall take what you leave. Let us see if there is justice upon earth.

"He cried and begged for mercy. But I drew my knife and held it to his throat. Finally he obeyed me. I swallowed the pill that was left. We both stood facing each other in silence—waiting to see who was to live and who was to die. Then I saw a look of horror on his face. He was feeling the first pangs of the poison. I laughed when I saw it. I held Lucy's marriage ring in front of his eyes. In a moment pain distorted his features. He threw up his hands, staggered, and fell heavily to the floor. I turned him over with my foot and placed my hand on his heart. There was no movement. He was dead!

"As I said, my nose had been bleeding. I don't know why I wrote upon the wall. Perhaps it was to set the police on the wrong track. I remembered that a German had been found dead in New York and the word RACHE was written above him. The meaning of the word had been much argued in the newspapers. I guessed that what puzzled New Yorkers would puzzle Londoners. So I dipped my finger in my own blood and wrote it on the wall. Then I walked down to my cab. I drove some distance before I realized Lucy's ring was gone. I was thunderstruck. It was all I had of her. I drove back to see if I dropped it over Drebber's body. I left the cab in a side street and walked boldly up to the house. I was willing to risk anything rather than lose Lucy's ring. I walked right into the arms of a police officer. I only managed to escape his suspicions by pretending to be drunk.

"That was how Enoch Drebber came to his end. Half the debt was paid. Stangerson was next. I went to Halliday's Private Hotel. I hung about there all day, but he never came out. He must have suspected something was wrong when Drebber did not show up and was hiding indoors. I found out which window was his. Early the next morning I climbed up a ladder to his room. I woke him up and told him his time had come to answer for the life he had taken so long ago. I described Drebber's death to him and I gave him the same choice of pills. But he did not grasp at the chance of safety I offered him. He sprang from his bed and flew at my throat. In self-defense I stabbed him. It would have been the same in any case, for I am sure fate would have guided his guilty hand to the poisoned pill.

"I went on driving the cab. I intended to keep at it until I could save enough to return to America. I was standing in the yard when a ragged youngster asked if there was a cabby there named Jefferson Hope. He said his cab was wanted by a gentleman at 221B Baker Street. I went around, suspecting no harm. The next thing I knew, this young man here had handcuffs on my wrists. That's the whole of my story, gentlemen. You may think that I am a murderer, but I believe I am as much an officer of justice as are you."

When he was finished, we all sat silent for some minutes. The only sound was the scratching of Lestrade's pencil as he took notes.

"There is only one point on which I should like a little more information," Sherlock Holmes said at last. "Who came for the ring I advertised?"

The prisoner winked at Sherlock. "I can tell my own

secrets," he said, "but I don't get other people into trouble. I saw your advertisement. I thought it might be a trap, or it might be the ring I wanted. My friend volunteered to go and see. I think you'll agree he did it smartly."

"Not a doubt of that," said Holmes, heartily.

"Now, gentlemen," the Inspector said gravely, "the prisoner will be brought to trial on Thursday. Your attendance will be required. Until then, I will be responsible for him." He rang a bell and Jefferson Hope was led off by two wardens. Sherlock Holmes and I then left the station and took a cab back to Baker Street.

Chapter 7
The Conclusion

There was no need for us to go to court on Thursday. A higher Judge had taken the matter in hand. Hope's artery burst the very night after his capture. He was found in the morning stretched upon the floor of the cell. A smile was on his face.

"Gregson and Lestrade will be very upset at his death. A trial would have been a good advertisement for Scotland Yard," Sherlock remarked the next evening.

"I don't see that they had much to do with his capture," I answered.

"They didn't. But they will take the credit. There is

little I can do. Never mind," he continued more brightly. "I would not have missed the investigation for anything. I cannot remember a better case. Simple as it was, there were some very instructive points about it."

"Simple!" I exclaimed.

"Well, really, it can hardly be described as otherwise," said Sherlock. "Yes, without any help except a few very ordinary deductions, I was able to capture the criminal within three days."

"That is true," said I.

"In solving a problem of this sort, the important thing is to be able to reason backward. That is a very useful skill and a very easy one. But people don't practice it much. In everyday life it is more useful to reason forward.

"You see, if you describe a train of events to most people they can tell you what should happen next. There are few people, however, who if you tell them what has come to pass, can tell you the steps that led up to it.

"Now this was a case in which we had the result and we had to find everything else out for ourselves. Now I will show you how I reasoned backward. As you know, I approached the house on foot. My mind was free from impressions. I naturally began by examining the street. I saw clearly the marks of a cab. Through inquiry, I learned that they must have been made during the night. I knew it was a cab rather than a private carriage by the size of the wheel marks.

"This was the first point I learned. I then walked slowly down the garden path. It happened to be made of a clay soil and so impressions showed well. To you it probably looked like a trampled mess, but to my trained eyes every mark had meaning. There is no branch of the detective service which is so important and so neglected as the art of tracing footsteps. I have always laid great stress on it. Much practice has made it second nature to me. I saw the heavy footprints of the police, but I also saw the tracks of two men. It was easy to separate them from the others. In places the marks were rubbed out by the others being on top. And so I now knew that two men had come by cab. One was remarkable for his height (which I figured from the length of his stride) and one was fashionably dressed (which I figured from the small and elegant impression of his boot).

"This deduction was confirmed on entering the house. My well-booted man lay before me. The tall one therefore had done the murder—if it was indeed murder. There was no wound on the body. But the agitated look on his face told me that he had seen his death coming. Now, men who die of heart disease and such do not have the chance to become so agitated. Their deaths are sudden. So I sniffed the man's lips. I detected a slightly sour smell and came to the conclusion that he had had poison forced upon him. Again, I reasoned that it had been forced upon him from the hatred and fear upon his face . . . no other answer fit the facts. This is not an unheard of idea. Poison being forced upon a victim is by no means a new thing in the history of crime. The cases of Dolska in Odessa, and of Leturier in Montpellier immediately come to mind.

"And now came the great question as to the reason why. Robbery had not been the object of the murder, as nothing was taken. Was it politics, then or a woman? That was the question which confronted me. Political assassins do their work quickly and flee. This murder had been done thoughtfully and the tracks in the room showed that the murderer had remained there all the time. It must have been a private wrong and not a political one. The inscription on the wall convinced me of this. It was too obviously meant to put us off the scent. When the ring was found, it settled the question. Clearly, the murderer had used it to remind his victim of some dead or absent woman. It was at this point that I asked Gregson about his telegram to Cleveland. I wanted to know if he had inquired about any particular point in Drebber's life. He answered no.

"I then proceeded to make a careful examination of the room. This confirmed my opinion about the murderer's height. It also gave me some new information, like the cigar and the length of his nails. Since there were no signs of a struggle, I had already come to the conclusion that the blood on the floor came from the murderer's nose. I could see that the trail of blood was the same as the track of his feet. Usually only full-blooded men break out in this way through emotion, which led me to think he was a robust and ruddy-faced man. Events proved that I had judged correctly.

"When I left the house, I did what Gregson had neglected to do. I telegraphed the head of police in Cleveland and asked about circumstances connected with the marriage of Enoch Drebber. The answer explained the situation. It told that Drebber had already applied for police protection against an old rival in love, named Jefferson Hope. It also stated that Hope was now in

Europe. I knew now that I held the clue to the mystery in my hand. All that remained was to capture the murderer.

"I had already decided that the cabdriver and the murderer were one and the same. The marks in the road showed me that the horse had wandered. This would not have been possible had someone been in charge of it. Where, then, could the driver be, unless he were inside the house? Again, a man would not carry out a crime right under the eyes of a witness . . . someone who was sure to betray him. Lastly, suppose a man wished to follow another through London. What better way than to become a cabdriver. All these deductions led me to believe that Mr. Jefferson Hope was to be found among the cabbies of London.

"There was no reason to think that he ceased to be one. On the contrary, any sudden change would draw attention to him. And there was no reason to suppose he was using a false name. Why should he change his name in a country where no one knew his original one? I organized my little street gang and sent them to every cab company in London. Eventually they found our man. The result of their finding, and how quickly I moved on it, must still be fresh in your mind. The murder of Stangerson was an unexpected incident. But it could not have been prevented. Through it, I came into the possession of the pills. As you know, I had already imagined their existence. You see, the whole thing is a chain of logical steps without a break or flaw."

"It is wonderful!" I cried. "Your merits should be publicly recognized. You should publish an account of the case. If you won't, I shall."

"You may do what you like, Doctor," Holmes said, as

he looked down at a newspaper. "See here!" he suddenly exclaimed and handed the paper to me. It said:

THE PUBLIC HAVE LOST A SENSATIONAL TREAT THROUGH THE SUDDEN DEATH OF JEFFERSON HOPE. HOPE WAS SUSPECTED OF THE MURDER OF MR. ENOCH DREBBER AND OF MR. JOSEPH STANGERSON. THE DETAILS OF THE CASE WILL PROBABLY NEVER BE KNOWN NOW. IT IS BELIEVED THE CRIME HAD TO DO WITH AN OLD-STANDING FEUD. LOVE AND MORMONISM ARE RUMORED TO HAVE PLAYED A PART. IT SEEMS THE VICTIMS WERE ONCE MOR-MONS AND ALL THREE MEN ONCE LIVED IN SALT LAKE CITY, UTAH, U.S.A. WHATEVER ITS OUTCOME, THE CASE SHOWS ONCE AGAIN THE EFFICIENCY OF OUR DETECTIVE POLICE FORCE. IT IS AN OPEN SECRET THAT THE CREDIT OF THE CAPTURE BELONGS TO THE WELL-KNOWN SCOTLAND YARD OFFICIALS MR. LESTRADE AND MR. GREG-SON. THE MAN WAS SEIZED IN THE ROOMS OF A CERTAIN MR. SHERLOCK HOLMES. MR. HOLMES IS AN AMATEUR WHO HAS SHOWN SOME SIGNS OF TALENT IN THE DETECTIVE LINE. WITH INSTRUCTORS LIKE LESTRADE AND GREGSON HE MAY SOME-DAY REACH THEIR LEVEL OF SKILL. AN AWARD IS TO BE GIVEN TO THE TWO OFFICERS FOR THEIR EXCELLENT SERVICES.

"Didn't I tell you so when we started?" cried Sherlock Holmes with a laugh. "That's what comes of our study in scarlet. Lestrade and Gregson receive awards!"

"Never mind!" I answered. "I have all the facts in my journal. The public will one day know of the great detective genius of Mr. Sherlock Holmes."

The
Red-headed
League

Conan Doyle's first two Sherlock Holmes stories may not have been sensations, but his short stories that followed were! Conan Doyle had come up with a brand-new idea in English literature—to present a series of short stories, all featuring the same character. The *Strand* magazine of London agreed to publish six such short stories, which Conan Doyle called "adventures." In a matter of months he had written all six. Among them was the adventure of *The Red-headed League*. It is said that he wrote the story in just ten days!

When the adventures began to appear in the *Strand* magazine its readership soared. The public loved Conan Doyle's clever new detective. And they loved following the adventures of Sherlock Holmes in the monthly magazine.

The Red-headed League

Last autumn I visited my friend, Mr. Sherlock Holmes, in the rooms we used to share at 221B Baker Street, London. I found him deep in conversation with a very stout, ruddy-faced gentleman with fiery red hair. I was about to leave when Holmes pulled me into the sitting room and closed the door behind me.

"You could not possibly have come at a better time, my dear Watson," he said cordially. "Mr. Jabez Wilson here has been telling me a most interesting story. Perhaps, Mr. Wilson, you would repeat your tale, so that Dr. Watson can hear it from the beginning and I can acquaint myself with every detail of the case. As a rule, after I've heard the basic facts, I can guide myself by the thousands of other similar cases set in my memory. But I must admit, your tale is unique."

The red-headed client puffed out his chest in pride and pulled a dirty and wrinkled newspaper from the inside pocket of his coat.

As he glanced down the advertisement column, I took a good look at him and tried to learn something from his dress and manner . . . as my friend Sherlock was so skilled at doing. However, I did not learn much. He looked like a typical English tradesman. He wore rather baggy check trousers and a not-too-clean black coat which was unbuttoned in the front. Beneath was a drab waistcoat from which a heavy brass watch chain and a square bit of metal dangled. A frayed top hat and faded brown overcoat with a wrinkled velvet collar lay on a chair beside him. Altogether, there was nothing very remarkable about the man except his blazing red head!

Sherlock Holmes' quick eye soon took in my occupation. Answering my thoughts, he said, "Beyond the obvious—that he has done manual labor at some time, that he has been in China, and that he has done a considerable amount of writing lately—I can deduce nothing at all."

With that, Mr. Jabez Wilson started up in his chair. His forefinger was still on the newspaper column, but his eyes were set on my companion.

"How did you know all that, Mr. Holmes?" he asked. "How did you know, for example, that I did manual labor? It's true as Gospel, for I began as a ship's carpenter!"

"Your hands, my dear sir. Your right hand is a size larger than your left. You have worked hard with it and so the muscles are more developed."

"Well, the writing then?"

"What else can be indicated by your right coat-cuff being so very shiny and your left coat-elbow so very smooth, where you must rest it on the desk."

"And China?"

"The fish you have tattooed above your right wrist could only have been done in China. I have made a small study of tattoo marks and have even contributed to literature on the subject. That trick of staining the fish scales a delicate pink is quite peculiar to China. When in addition I see a Chinese coin hanging from your watch chain, the matter becomes even more simple."

Mr. Jabez Wilson laughed heartily. "Well, I never!" he said. "I thought at first that you were very clever, but now I see there was nothing to your deductions after all!"

Holmes turned toward me. "I begin to think, Watson, that I make a mistake explaining my reasoning. I must protect my reputation!" Then turning back to his client he said, "Can you find the advertisement?"

"Yes, I have it now," Wilson answered, his thick red finger planted halfway down the column. "Here it is. This is what began it all. You can read it for yourselves."

I took the paper from him and read the following words:

TO THE RED-HEADED LEAGUE:

THERE IS NOW ANOTHER VACANCY OPEN WHICH ENTITLES A MEMBER OF THE LEAGUE TO A SALARY OF FOUR POUNDS A WEEK FOR LIGHT SERVICES. ALL RED-HEADED MEN WHO ARE SOUND IN BODY AND MIND AND ABOVE THE AGE OF TWENTY-ONE ARE ELIGIBLE. APPLY IN PERSON ON MONDAY AT ELEVEN O'CLOCK TO DUNCAN ROSS AT THE OFFICES OF THE LEAGUE, ROOM NUMBER FOUR, 17 POPES COURT, FLEET STREET, LONDON.

"What on earth does it mean?" I exclaimed in amazement.

Holmes chuckled and wriggled in his chair, as was his habit in high spirits. "It is a little off the beaten track, isn't it?" he said. "And now, Mr. Wilson, tell us about yourself, your household, and the effect this advertisement had upon your fortunes."

"I have a small pawnbroker's business at Saxe-Coburg Square near the business district," Mr. Jabez Wilson began. "It's not a very large enterprise. Lately it's barely provided me with a living. I used to keep two assistants, but now I keep only one and I'd be hard put to pay him his full wages. Luckily, he is willing to work for half-pay so as to learn the business."

"What is the name of this obliging youth?" asked Holmes.

"His name is Vincent Spaulding and he's not such a youth. I could not wish for a smarter assistant. He could earn twice what I pay him elsewhere. But if he is satisfied, why should I put ideas in his head?"

"Why, indeed?" asked Holmes. "You seem most fortunate in having an employee who comes under the market price. It is not a common experience among employees these days. I don't know that your assistant isn't as remarkable as your advertisement."

"Oh, he has his faults," said Mr. Wilson. "He loves photography. He's always snapping away with his camera and diving down into the cellar, like a rabbit into a hole, to develop his pictures. That's his main fault. But he's a good worker."

"He is still with you, I presume?"

"Yes, sir. He and a girl of fourteen who does a bit of simple cooking and keeps the place clean. That's all I have in the house. I am a widower and never had any family. The three of us live very quietly. We keep a roof over our heads and pay our debts, if nothing more.

"Then eight weeks ago Spaulding came down into the office with this very paper in his hand, saying: 'I wish, Mr. Wilson, that I was a red-headed man. Here's another vacancy on the League of Red-headed Men. I understand there are more vacancies than there are men to fill them. The trustees are at their wits end what to do with all the money!'

" 'What's this?' I asked him.

" 'Why, have you never heard of the League of Red-headed Men?'

" 'Never!'

" 'Why, I wonder at that, for you are eligible yourself. They pay a couple of hundred pounds a year, the work is slight and need not interfere with one's usual business.'

"Well, that made my ears prick up. As I said, business has not been good and the extra money would be helpful. So I asked him to tell me about it.

" 'Well,' he replied, showing me the advertisement, 'you can see for yourself. The League has a vacancy and there is the address where you should apply. As far as I can make out, the League was founded by an American millionaire named Ezekiah Hopkins. He was red-headed and had a great sympathy for all red-headed men. When he died, he left an enormous fortune in the hands of trustees. They were instructed to help out needy men with the same hair color as was his.'

" 'But there are millions of red-headed men who could apply,' I interrupted.

" 'Not so many as you might think,' he answered. 'I have heard that it is no use applying if you have light or dark red hair. Or any other color but bright, blazing, fiery red.'

"Now," continued Mr. Wilson, "my hair is a very full and rich tint as you can see. It seemed to me that I stood as good a chance as any in such a competition. So since it was Monday—the day for applying—Vincent and I quickly shut up shop and started off for the address in the advertisement.

"Well, you've never seen so many red-headed men. The area was packed with red-headed folk. Every shade of color was there: straw, lemon, orange, brick, Irish setter, liver, clay. But not many had truly vivid red hair like mine. Somehow Vincent pushed and pulled and butted through the crowd right up to the office steps. We soon found ourselves inside.

"There was nothing in the office but a couple of wooden chairs and a card table. Behind the table sat a small man with a head even redder than mine. There were other candidates in the room but he managed to find fault with each. However, when my turn came he exclaimed, 'I cannot recall when I have seen anything so fine!' He took a step backward, cocked his head to one side, and stared at my head. Then he plunged suddenly forward, shook my hand and congratulated me on my success. Then he stopped, added, 'One last precaution!' and seized my hair in both his hands and tugged till I yelled in pain. 'There is water in your eyes,' he said happily as he released me. 'I see all is as it should be!' He stepped over to the window and shouted that the position had been filled. The crowd gave a groan of disappointment and trooped away until there was not a red head to be seen except that of the manager and my own.

"The job involved remaining in the office from ten to two o'clock each morning. I was to copy the Encyclopaedia Britannica. Now, a pawnbroker's business is mostly in the evenings so it suited me well to earn a little extra in the morning. Besides, I knew my assistant could handle any problems that came up in the shop. I had to supply the ink, pens, and blotting paper, while Mr. Ross provided the table and chair.

" 'Could you be ready to start tomorrow?' the manager asked.

" 'Certainly,' I answered, and went home very pleased at my good fortune. But later that night I began to worry about the entire affair. I felt sure it was some kind of strange hoax. Still, in the morning I decided to go and see for myself. I bought a penny bottle of ink, a quill pen, and seven sheets of paper and went to the office of the Red-headed League.

"Sure enough, there was Mr. Ross! He soon started me off with the letter A. From time to time he dropped in to see how I was getting on. This went on day after day. I never dared leave the office for fear he might drop in at any moment. On Saturday he came in and plunked down four golden coins in payment for my week's work. It was the same the next week and the week after. Eight weeks passed like this and I wrote about Abbotts and Archery and Armor and Architecture and hoped to be onto the Bs before too long. I had filled a shelf with my writings when suddenly the whole business came to an end."

"Came to an end?" questioned Sherlock.

"Yes, sir. This very morning. I went to work as usual to find the door shut and locked. A little square of cardboard was hammered onto it. You can read it yourself."

He held it up for us to read. It said:

THE RED-HEADED LEAGUE IS DISSOLVED
OCT. 9, 1890

Sherlock Holmes and I looked at the brief announcement and the disappointed face behind it. Suddenly the whole matter seemed so funny that we burst out laughing.

"I cannot see that there is anything very funny about it!" cried our client, rising from his chair. "If you can do nothing better than laugh at me, I can go elsewhere!"

"No, no!" assured Sherlock, shoving the man back into his chair. "I really wouldn't miss this case for the world. It is most refreshingly unusual. But there really is something comical about it. Now, what did you do upon finding this note?"

"I was staggered, sir. I did not know what to do. I inquired about it at the offices on the floor but they knew nothing. So I went to the landlord on the ground floor and asked him what had become of the Red-headed League. He said he had never heard of such an organization. Nor had he heard of the manager, Mr. Duncan Ross.

" 'Well,' said I, 'what about the gentleman in room number four?'

" 'The red-headed man? His name was William Morris,' he replied. 'He was a lawyer and was using number four as a temporary office until his new one was ready. He moved out yesterday. I believe his new address is 17 King Edward Street.'

"So I went to that address. It was a company that manufactured artificial kneecaps. No one worked there named Morris or Ross."

"And what did you do next?" asked Holmes.

"I went home and asked the opinion of my assistant. He thought I would probably hear by post. But that was not good enough, Mr. Holmes. I did not wish to lose such a good-paying job without a struggle. I had heard that you gave advice to poor folk in need of it. So I came to you."

"And you did very wisely," said Holmes. "From what you have told me I think graver issues are involved in this case than one would suspect!"

"Grave enough!" said Mr. Jabez Wilson. "Why, I have lost four pounds a week!"

"As far as you are personally concerned," remarked Holmes, "you should have no grievance with this extraordinary league. On the contrary, you are some thirty pounds richer because of it. To say nothing of the minute knowledge you have gained on every subject starting with the letter A. You have lost nothing!"

"No, sir. But I want to find out more about it. Who are they and what was their object in playing a prank on me, if it was a prank . . ."

"We shall endeavor to clear up these points for you. But first a few questions. How long had your assistant worked for you at the time of the advertisement?"

"About a month."

"And how did he come to you?"

"He came in answer to an advertisement I placed in the newspaper."

"Was he the only applicant?"

"No, I had a dozen."

"Why did you pick him?"

"Because he was handy and would come cheap."

"At half-wages, in fact?"

"Yes."

"What is he like, this Vincent Spaulding?"

"Small, stout, but very quick in his ways," replied Wilson. "He has no hair on his face but must be close to thirty. He has a mark on his forehead from a splash of acid."

Holmes suddenly sat up in his chair in considerable excitement.

"I thought as much! Is one of his ears pierced?"

"Yes! He told me that a gypsy pierced it for him when he was a lad."

"Hum!" exclaimed Holmes. "Is he still with you?"

"Oh yes, sir! I have only just left him."

"And has your business been attended to properly in your absence?"

"Nothing to complain of, sir. There's never much to do in the mornings."

"I shall be happy to give you an opinion on the subject in a day or two," Holmes said. "Today is Saturday. I hope to have solved the mystery by Monday."

"Well, Watson, what do you make of it all?" Sherlock asked me after his client had left.

"I make nothing of it," I answered frankly. "What are you going to do?"

"To smoke. It is quite a three-pipe problem. I beg you not to speak to me for fifty minutes." He then curled himself up in his armchair with his knees drawn up to his hawklike nose. There he sat contemplating the matter with his black pipe thrusting out like the bill of some strange bird. Just as I was nodding off and thought he was as well, he suddenly sprang up from his chair and put his pipe down on the mantel.

"There is a good concert at the auditorium in the Strand this afternoon. We can go through the business district on our way!" In moments he had gathered up our coats and was pushing me out the door.

It was not long before we arrived at Saxe-Coburg Square where Mr. Wilson lived and worked. It was a shabby street with rows of two-story brick houses looking out on an enclosed park where a lawn of weedy grass and a few clumps of faded bushes struggled for survival. Above a corner house hung a board on which was lettered in white the name JABEZ WILSON. Sherlock Holmes looked it all over, walked across the street and then back to the corner, always keeping an eye on the pawnbroker's shop. Then he walked right up to it and pounded the pavement with his stick. Finally he went up to the door and knocked. It was instantly opened by a bright-looking, clean-shaven young man who invited him in.

"Thank you," said Holmes. "I only wish to ask you the way from here to the Strand."

"Third right, fourth left," answered the assistant and closed the door.

"Smart fellow, that," observed Holmes as we walked away. "He is, in my judgment, the fourth smartest man in

London and for daring he might be the third. I have known something of him before."

"It seems so," I replied. "Mr. Wilson's assistant obviously plays a key role in the League. You asked directions, then, to observe him."

"Not him. The knees of his trousers."

"And what did you see?"

"What I expected to see."

"Why did you beat the pavement?"

"My dear Watson, this is a time for observation, not talk. We are spies in an enemy's country! Now that we know something of Saxe-Coburg Square, let us explore the area behind it."

The road behind Saxe-Coburg was much its opposite. It was a main thoroughfare with heavy traffic and swarms of pedestrians walking past the fine shops and business offices.

"Let me see," said Holmes, standing at the corner. "I should like to remember the exact order of the houses here. It's a hobby of mine to have an exact knowledge of London. There is Mortimer's—the tobacconist, the little newspaper shop, the Coburg branch of the City and Suburban Bank, the Vegetarian restaurant, and McFarlane's Carriage-building Depot. And now, Doctor, since our business is done, let us go."

After the concert Holmes said, "You want to go home, no doubt, Watson. I have some business to attend to which will take some hours. This business at Saxe-Coburg Square is serious."

"Why serious?"

"A considerable crime is in contemplation. I have

every reason to believe we shall be in time to stop it. But today is Saturday, which complicates matters. I shall want your help tonight. Ten o'clock should be early enough."

"Then I shall be at Baker Street at ten," I replied.

"And I say, Doctor! There may be some little danger," Sherlock added. "Kindly put your army revolver in your pocket." He waved his hands, turned on his heel, and instantly disappeared into the crowd.

That night I found two hansom cabs waiting outside Holmes' house. Within I discovered Holmes deep in conversation with two men.

"Ha, our party is now complete!" exclaimed Holmes on seeing me. He buttoned his pea jacket and took up his riding crop. "Watson, I think you know Mr. Jones of Scotland Yard? Let me introduce you to Mr. Merryweather, who is to be our companion on tonight's adventure."

"This is the first Saturday in twenty-seven years that I shall miss my card game," he muttered. "I do hope it is not in vain."

"I think you will find," replied Holmes, "that you will be playing for a higher stake tonight than you have ever before. For you, Mr. Merryweather, the stake will be some 30,000 pounds. And for you, Mr. Jones, it will be the man you wish to lay your hands on . . ."

"John Clay, the murderer, thief, and forger," said Jones of Scotland Yard. "He's young but at the head of his profession. I would rather have my handcuffs on him than any other criminal in London. I've been on his track for years and have never set eyes on him!"

"I hope I may have the pleasure of introducing you tonight," remarked Holmes. "It is past ten and time we started. If you two will take the first cab, Watson and I will follow in the second."

Holmes did not speak until we were close to our destination. Finally he said, "This fellow Merryweather is a bank director and personally interested in this matter. I thought it as well to have Jones with us also. He's not a bad fellow, though an absolute imbecile at his profession. Still, he's brave as a bulldog and once he has his claws on someone he holds on tight. Here we are and they are waiting for us."

We had arrived at the same busy thoroughfare we had visited earlier that day. After we dismissed the cabs, Mr. Merryweather led us down a narrow passage, through a side door, and into a small corridor. At its end was a massive iron gate. Beyond was a flight of winding stone steps and at their base yet another gate. Mr. Merryweather then stopped to light a lantern before leading us down a dark, earth-smelling passage to a huge vault or cellar. Crates and massive boxes were piled high.

"You are not very vulnerable from above," Holmes said, looking up.

"Nor from below," said Mr. Merryweather. And he struck his stick on the flagstone floor. "Why, dear me, it sounds quite hollow!" he exclaimed in surprise.

"I must ask you to be a little more quiet," said Holmes severely. "You have already endangered the success of our expedition. Please sit down on one of these boxes and do not interfere."

The solemn Mr. Merryweather perched himself on a crate with a very injured expression on his face. Meanwhile, Sherlock Holmes got down on his knees and

pulled a large magnifying glass from his pocket. He then
examined the cracks between the floor-stones. After a few
seconds he got back on his feet and put the magnifying
glass away.

"We have at least an hour to wait," he remarked.
"They can hardly act until the good pawnbroker is safely
in bed. Then they will move quickly. The sooner they do
their work, the more time they will have for their escape!
As you may have figured out, Watson, we are at present in
the cellar of the Coburg branch of one of the principal
London banks. Mr. Merryweather is the chairman of the
bank directors. He will explain to you why some of the
most daring criminals in London should be interested in
this particular cellar."

"It is our French gold," whispered the director. "We
have had several warnings that an attempt might be made
upon it."

"Your French gold?" I asked.

"Yes. We recently had an opportunity to strengthen
our resources and so borrowed 30,000 gold napoleons
from the Bank of France. Unfortunately, it has become
known that the money has never been unpacked and that
it is still lying here in our cellar. The crate I am sitting on
right now contains 2000 napoleons packed between layers
of lead foil. Our reserve of bullion is much larger at
present than is usually kept in a single branch office. The
directors have had considerable misgivings about it."

"Which were very well justified," observed Holmes.
"And now it is time to arrange our plans. We must put the
screen down over the lantern."

"And sit in the dark?" Merryweather asked.

"I am afraid so. I brought a pack of cards and I thought since we were four you might have your game after all. But I see the enemy's preparations have gone too far. We cannot risk the presence of light. We must choose our positions. These are daring men. Even though we take them by surprise, they could still do us harm. I shall stand behind this crate. You conceal yourselves behind those. When I flash the light on them, close in swiftly. Watson, if they fire, do not hesitate to shoot!"

I placed my cocked revolver on the wooden crate in front of me. Holmes closed the screen on the lantern. We were in pitch darkness. The smell of hot metal remained. It reminded us that the light was still there, ready to flash out at a moment's notice.

"They have but one retreat," whispered Holmes. "Back through the house into Saxe-Coburg Square. I hope you have done what I asked, Jones?"

"I have an inspector and two officers waiting at the front door."

"Then we have stopped all the holes. Now we must be silent and wait."

What a time it seemed! It was actually only an hour and a quarter but it seemed like the entire night had passed. My limbs were weary and stiff, but I dared not shift position. My nerves were on end. My hearing was so acute that I could distinguish between the deeper, heavier breath of the bulky Jones and the thin sighing breath of the bank director. Then suddenly the wait was over and my eyes caught sight of a glint of light.

At first it was just a spark in the cracks of the floorstones. Then it lengthened out and became a yellow light. Then without warning, a gash seemed to open and a white, almost womanly hand appeared. Suddenly a rending, tearing sound could be heard. One of the broad white stones turned over on its side. It left a square, gaping hole. Light shone through. Over the edge peered a clean-cut, boyish face. He looked about and then drew himself up and into the cellar. In another instant he was hauling his companion up as well. The companion was small and pale as well with a shock of very red hair.

"It's all clear," the first rogue whispered. "Have you the chisel and the bag? Great Scott! Jump, Archie, jump!"

Sherlock Holmes had opened the light, sprung out and seized the first intruder by the collar. The other dived down the hole. I heard the sound of ripping cloth as Jones clutched at his coattails. The light exposed the barrel of a revolver, but Holmes' hunting crop came down on the man's wrist. The pistol clinked on the stone floor.

"It's no use, John Clay!" said Holmes. "You have no chance at all!"

"So I see," the other answered with the utmost coolness. "I guess my friend at least got away . . . though I see you have his coattails."

"There are three men waiting for him at the pawnbroker's front door," said Holmes blandly.

"Indeed! You seem to have done the thing very completely. I must compliment you."

"And I you," Holmes answered. "Your red-headed idea was very new and effective."

Jones placed his handcuffs on John Clay and marched him upstairs. A cab was waiting to take him and his red-headed accomplice to the police station.

"Really, Mr. Holmes," said Mr. Merryweather. "I do not know how the bank can thank you or repay you. There is no doubt you have detected and defeated one of the most determined attempts at bank robbery ever!"

"I have had one or two little scores of my own to settle with Mr. John Clay," said Sherlock Holmes. "The matter cost me a small amount which I shall expect the bank to refund. But beyond that, I am amply repaid by having had a unique experience and for hearing the very remarkable tale of the Red-headed League."

"You see, Watson," Holmes explained back at Baker Street, "it was perfectly obvious to me that the purpose of the Red-headed League was to get the pawnbroker out of the way a number of hours each day. It was a curious way of managing it, but really it would be difficult to suggest one better. The method was no doubt suggested to Clay's ingenious mind by the color of both his accomplice's and his employer's hair. The four pounds a week was a lure to draw the pawnbroker out of his shop. What was four pounds a week when they were after thousands? They first placed the advertisement in the newspaper. Then Ross-Morris rented a temporary office while Clay persuaded his boss to apply for the position. Together they managed to get the pawnbroker out of his shop each morning. From the moment I heard that the assistant worked for half-pay, I knew he had some strong motive for wanting that job."

"But how could you guess what that motive was?"

"The man's business was a small one, and there was nothing in his house of great value to steal. What did these two rogues want then? It must be something outside the house. I thought of the assistant's fondness for photography and his habit of vanishing into the cellar. The cellar! There was the clue! I made inquiries into this mysterious assistant and recognized his description. I was dealing with one of the coolest and most daring criminals in London! He was doing something in the cellar. . . . Something which took many hours each day for weeks on end. What could it be? The only thing I could think of was that he was running a tunnel to some other building.

"That is as far as I got when we visited Saxe-Coburg Square. I surprised you by beating on the pavement with my stick. I was trying to find out whether the cellar stretched in front or behind the building. It was not in front. I then rang the bell. As I hoped, the assistant answered it. We have had some near encounters, but we have never set eyes on each other before. I hardly looked into his face. His knees were what I wished to see. You must yourself have noticed how worn, wrinkled, and stained they were. They spoke of those long hours of digging. But what were they digging for? I walked around the corner. The City and Suburban Bank abutted the pawnbroker's shop. I felt sure I had solved the case. When you drove home after the concert, I called on Scotland Yard and the chairman of the bank directors. You witnessed the result."

"And how could you tell that they would make their attempt tonight?" I asked.

"Well, they closed their League offices. That was a sign that they no longer needed Mr. Wilson out of the house. In other words, they had completed their tunnel. But they had to use it as quickly as possible—before it was discovered or the bullion was removed. Saturday was the best choice of days as the bank was closed and they would have the weekend to make their escape. For all these reasons I expected them to come tonight."

"You reasoned it out beautifully!" I exclaimed in admiration. "It is so long a chain and yet every link rings true."

"Elementary, my dear Watson, elementary," replied Mr. Sherlock Holmes.

The Man with the Twisted Lip

Conan Doyle had agreed to write six adventures for the *Strand* magazine. *The Man with the Twisted Lip* was the last of these. But Holmes had become the rage and it was not long before the editors of the magazine and its readers were begging Conan Doyle for more!

The Man with the Twisted Lip was quite unlike the five earlier short stories. Its opening in the opium den and the subject of begging were and still are controversial topics. But it featured Holmes, and so despite its unusual subject matter it was eagerly read by all.

The Man with the
Twisted Lip

Mr. Isa Whitney was addicted to opium. It seems that in college he tried it and found that the practice was easier to start than to stop. And so for many years he was a slave to the drug. I can see him now with his yellow, pasty face and drooping eyelids, sitting all huddled up in a chair. He had become the wreck and ruin of a man.

One night in June 1889 there was a ring at my bell. I sat up in my chair. My wife laid down her needlework and made a face of disappointment.

"A patient!" she said. "Now, you'll have to go out."

I groaned, for I was tired from a busy day.

Our housekeeper let the visitor in and there was the sound of footsteps on the stair. A woman entered the room. She was darkly dressed and wore a black veil over her face.

"You will excuse my calling so late," the lady said. Then suddenly she ran forward and threw her arms around my wife's neck. "Oh, I'm in such trouble!" she cried. "I need your help!"

My wife pulled up the lady's veil. There was her old schoolfriend, Kate Whitney. "Why, Kate," she said. "How you startled me! I had no idea it was you."

"I didn't know what to do, so I came straight to you."

"You must have some wine and water and sit here

comfortably and tell us all about it. Or would you prefer John to leave?"

"No, no, no," my wife's old schoolfriend said. "I want the Doctor's advice and help too. It's about Isa. He hasn't come home in two days. I am so frightened for him."

It was not the first time she had spoken to us of her husband's problem—to me as a doctor and to my wife as a friend. We soothed her and comforted her as best we could. We asked her if she knew where her husband was. Was it possible that we could bring him back to her?

It seemed it was. She said that he often went to a lowly opium den in the city. He usually stayed a few hours and always came back home. But now he had been gone forty-eight hours. She feared he lay in that vile place sleeping or sick. It was by the docks and was called The Bar of Gold. But what was she to do? How could she—a young and timid woman—go to such a place? How could she get her husband away from there?

It was decided that I should go alone. I promised to send Isa home in a cab within two hours, if he indeed was there. And so in ten minutes my cosy armchair and cheery sitting room were far behind me. I was speeding in a cab eastward on a strange errand. Only the future would prove how truly strange it was to be.

I found the opium den in an alleyway by the river. I ordered my cab to wait, walked down the stairs, and made my way into a long, low room. It was thick and heavy with brown opium smoke.

As I entered, an attendant rushed up to me with a pipe filled with the drug.

"Thank you, I have not come to stay," said I. "There is

a friend of mine here, Mr. Isa Whitney, and I wish to speak with him."

There was a movement and an exclamation to my right. I looked over and saw Whitney staring at me.

"My God! It's Watson," he said. "I say, Watson, what time is it?"

"Nearly eleven," I answered.

"Of what day?"

"Of Friday, June 19."

"Good heavens! I thought it was Wednesday. It *is* Wednesday. What d'you want to frighten a chap for?" he said.

"I tell you it is Friday, man. Your wife has been waiting for you for two days. You should be ashamed of yourself!"

"So I am but you're mixed-up, Watson. I have only been here for a few hours, three, four pipes—I forget how many. But I'll go home with you. I wouldn't frighten poor Kate. Give me your hand! Have you got a cab?"

"Yes, I have one waiting," I said as I helped him up.

"Then I shall go in it. But I must owe something. Find out what I owe, Watson. I can't do it myself."

I walked up a narrow passage looking for the manager. Suddenly, I felt a pluck at my coat. A low voice whispered, "Walk past me and then look back at me." I looked about. The words could only have come from an old man at my side. He was very thin, very wrinkled, and very bent with age. I took two steps forward and looked back. I had to stop myself from crying out in astonishment. He had turned his back so no one else could see him. His form had filled out, his wrinkles were gone. There, grinning at my surprise, was none other than Mr.

Sherlock Holmes. He made a slight motion for me to approach him. Instantly, he became the doddering, old man once more.

"Holmes!" I whispered. "What on earth are you doing in a place like this?"

"Speak as low as you can," he answered. "I have excellent ears. Can you send your friend home alone? I would like very much to speak with you."

"I have a cab outside."

"Then please send him home in it. I should also send a note with the cabdriver to your wife, saying that you have met up with me. If you will wait outside, I will be with you in five minutes."

I wrote my note, paid Whitney's bill, led him out to the cab and watched as he was driven off. Then I waited for my friend. The prospect of an adventure with Mr. Sherlock Holmes filled me with excitement.

In a very short time an old man emerged from the den. For two streets he shuffled along beside me. Then glancing around, he straightened himself and burst into a hearty fit of laughter.

"I suppose, Watson, you were surprised to see me in that den?" Holmes said.

"Yes, indeed," I answered.

"But no more so than I to see you," he replied.

"I came to find a friend."

"And I to find an enemy."

"An enemy?"

"Yes," answered Holmes seriously. "I am in the midst of a remarkable case. I hoped to find a clue at that den tonight. I had to be careful not to be recognized. I have had more than one run-in with the owner. He has sworn to have vengeance on me. There is a trapdoor at the back of the building. It could tell some strange tales about what has passed through it in the dead of night."

"What! You don't mean bodies?"

"Aye, bodies, Watson. We would be rich men if we had a thousand pounds for every poor devil who has been murdered there. That den is the vilest murder-trap along the river. I fear that Neville St. Clair has entered it never to leave it again. Now, Watson, my carriage is nearby. You'll come with me, won't you?"

"If I can be of use," I answered.

"Oh, a trusty comrade is always of use. My room at The Cedars is a double-bedded one."

"The Cedars?"

"Yes, that is Mr. St. Clair's house. I am staying there while I conduct the inquiry."

"Where is it, then?" I asked.

"Near Lee, in Kent. We have a seven-mile drive before us."

"But I am still in the dark."

"Of course you are. You'll know all about it presently."

We jumped up onto the carriage. He flicked the horse with his whip and in a moment we were dashing through the streets of London. In time the streets broadened, we crossed a bridge, and began to drive through the suburbs. All the while Holmes was silent. He seemed lost in thought. I was curious about this adventure, but I did not interrupt his thoughts. At last, he shook himself, shrugged his shoulders, and lit his pipe.

"You have a great gift of silence, Watson," he said. "It makes you quite an invaluable companion. It is a great thing for me to have someone to talk to. My own thoughts are not too pleasant. I was just wondering what I should say to Mrs. St. Clair."

"You forget that I know nothing about the case."

"I shall just have time to tell you the facts before we get to Lee. It seems absurdly simple, and yet I can find nothing to go on. Now I'll state the case clearly to you, Watson. Maybe you will see something that I have not."

"Proceed then," I said.

"In 1884 a gentleman by the name of Neville St. Clair came to Lee. He bought a villa and liv:d in good style. Eventually he made friends in the neighborhood. In 1887 he married the daughter of the local brewer. They now have two children. He had no particular occupation. But he was interested in several companies and went into town most mornings. He always returned by the 5:14 train. Mr. St. Clair is now 37 years of age, a good husband, an affectionate father, and popular with all. I may add that he is not indebted to anyone. There is no reason, therefore, to think that money troubles have been bothering him.

"Last Monday, Mr. Neville St. Clair went into town earlier than usual. He told his wife that he had two errands to run and would bring his little boy a box of blocks. After he left, his wife received a telegram. It said that a parcel she awaited had arrived in London. She could pick it up at the shipping company. As it happens, the company is located quite near the den where you found me tonight. Mrs. St. Clair had her lunch, started off for the city, and did some shopping. She then got her parcel and headed back toward the station. She was walking directly in front of the den at 4:35. Have you followed me so far?"

"It is very clear," I said.

"If you remember, Monday was an exceedingly hot day. Mrs. St. Clair was walking slowly down the street. She did not like the neighborhood she found herself in and so was glancing about looking for a cab. Suddenly she heard a cry or exclamation from above. She looked up and was astonished to see her husband looking down at her. He seemed to be beckoning to her from a second-floor window. The window was open, and she distinctly saw his face. She said he looked terribly upset. He waved his hands frantically to her. Then he vanished suddenly. It seemed to her that he had been pulled back into the room. One odd point she noticed: although he wore a dark coat, which looked like his own, he had neither collar nor necktie beneath.

"She was positive something was wrong. She rushed down the steps of the den, and ran into the front room. She then attempted to go up the stairs to the second floor. She was blocked by the owner who pushed her out into the street. She ran down the lane and by good luck met two policemen and an Inspector. They followed her back to the den. Despite the resistance of the owner, they made their way upstairs. There was no sign of St. Clair. In fact, there was no one to be found on that floor except a pitiful cripple who lived there. Both he and the owner swore that no one else had been in the front room all day. The Inspector was beginning to believe them when Mrs. St. Clair let out a cry. She had spotted a box on the table. She tore the lid from it. A cascade of children's blocks fell out.

It was the toy which her husband had promised to bring home.

"The cripple seemed confused at this point. The toy and his confusion made the Inspector realize that the matter was serious. The rooms were carefully examined. The results pointed to some terrible crime. The front room was plainly furnished as a sitting room. It led to a small back bedroom which looked out onto a wharf below. Between the wharf and the bedroom window is a narrow strip. This strip is dry at low tide but is covered at high tide by at least four and a half feet of water. The bedroom window was shut. There were traces of blood on its sill. Scattered drops of blood were on the floor. Behind a curtain they found the clothes of Neville St. Clair . . . except his coat. His boots, his socks, his hat—all were there. There were no signs of violence on the garments and there were no other traces of Neville St. Clair. He must have gone out the window, for there was no other exit. The blood indicated that he was wounded. The high tide and fast current at that time of day would have made it difficult for him to swim to safety.

"And now as to the two men who would seem to be villains. . . . The owner was known as an evil man, but as Mrs. St. Clair said, he was at the base of the stairs within seconds of her husband's appearance at the window. He pleaded ignorance. He said that he did not know anything of the missing gentleman's clothes, nor did he know about the doings of his crippled lodger, Mr. Hugh Boone.

"So much for the owner. Now, as to the cripple. His name is Hugh Boone. His hideous face is familiar to every man who works in the business district. He is a professional beggar. To avoid the police, he pretends to have a small business in matches. There is a small angle in the wall on Threadneedle Street. There, the beggar sits cross-legged each day. A tiny pile of matches is always in his lap. A greasy leather cap lies on the pavement beside him. He is so striking and pitiful to see that passersby drop coins into his hat all day long. He has a shock of orange hair, and a horrible scar which twists the corner of his upper lip. He has a bulldog chin, and a pair of penetrating dark eyes. He is also bright and always has a quick reply to those who would joke with him. This is the man who lives at the opium den. He was the last man to see Neville St. Clair alive."

"But a cripple!" said I. "How could he have single-handedly harmed a man in the prime of his life?"

"He is a cripple in that he walks with a limp. But in other respects he appears to be a powerful man. Surely your medical experience tells you that weakness in one limb is often made up for by strength in another."

"Pray continue your story," said I.

"Mrs. St. Clair fainted on seeing the blood on the windowsill. She was escorted home in a cab by the police. Inspector Barton, who was in charge of the case, inspected the rooms carefully and could not find any evidence. One mistake was made . . . he did not immediately arrest Boone. Boone therefore had a few minutes in which he could speak unnoticed with his friend the owner. However, this mistake was soon set straight and Boone was seized and searched. Nothing was found upon his body. Some bloodstains were found on his right shirtsleeve. This he explained by pointing to his right ring finger which was cut near the nail. He also added that he had been near the window and the blood on the sill could easily have come from his own finger. He swore that he had never seen Mr. Neville St. Clair, and argued that the clothes in his room were as much a mystery to him as they were to the police. He said that Mrs. St. Clair must have been mad or dreaming. Protesting loudly, he was taken to the police station. The Inspector remained at the den to wait for the tide to go out. He hoped the mudbank beneath would reveal some clue to the mystery.

"And it did, though hardly what they expected. Rather than finding the body of Neville St. Clair, they found his coat. And what do you think they found in his pockets?"

"I cannot imagine," said I.

"No, I don't think you could guess. Every pocket was stuffed with pennies. It was no wonder it had not been swept away by the tide. A human body, though, is a different matter. There is a fierce current between the wharf and the house. It is possible that a weighted coat would sink while a stripped body would be carried out into the river."

"But all the other clothes were found in the room. Would the body only be dressed in a coat? And the coat somehow stripped off him in the water?"

"No, but the facts can be fitted together. Suppose this man Boone thrust Neville St. Clair out the back window. No human eye could have seen the deed. What would he do then? He would have to get rid of the telltale garments. He'd seize the coat to throw it through the window. But then it would occur to him that the coat would float rather than sink. He'd hear the scuffle below between the owner and the wife and know he had little time. Perhaps the owner had already told him that police were scurrying up the street. He'd rush to some secret horde where he kept his beggar's pennies. He'd stuff the pockets of the coat with pennies and throw it out the window. He'd have done the same with the rest of the clothes when suddenly he hears footsteps on the stairs. He has time only to close the window before the police appear."

"It certainly sounds possible," I said.

"Well, we'll use the story for now, for want of something better. As I said, Boone was arrested and taken to the station. It turns out that he does not have a police record. It seems he has been known as a professional beggar for years, but his life has been a quiet and innocent one. There the matter stands. The questions to be solved now are: What was Neville St. Clair doing in an opium den? What happened to him while there? Where is he now? And what does Hugh Boone have to do with his disappearance? I confess that I cannot remember another case which at first looked so simple, and yet presented so many difficulties!"

Just as Sherlock Holmes finished his story, we drove through a village. A few lights glimmered in the windows.

"We are on the outskirts of Lee," he said. "See that light among the trees? That is The Cedars. Beside that lamp sits a woman whose anxious ears have already heard the clink of our horse's feet."

"But why are you not conducting the case from Baker Street?" I asked.

"Because there are many inquiries which must be made here. Mrs. St. Clair has given me two rooms to use, and I am sure she will welcome a friend of mine. I hate to see her, though, when I have no news of her husband. Here we are. Whoa, there, whoa!"

We had pulled up in front of a large villa. A stable boy ran out to assist us. We jumped down and walked up a winding, gravel drive toward the house. Suddenly the front door flew open. A little blonde woman dressed in pink chiffon stood at the opening.

"Well?" she cried. "Well? No good news?"

"None," Sherlock answered.

"No bad?" she asked.

"No."

"Thank God for that. But come in. You must be weary. You have had a long day."

"This is my friend, Dr. Watson," Holmes said. "He has been of most vital use to me in several of my cases."

"I am delighted to see you," she said, and shook my hand warmly.

We followed her into the dining room. A cold supper was laid out upon the table. "Now, Mr. Holmes," she said, as he seated himself in a chair, "I should very much like to ask you one or two plain questions. I beg that you give me a plain answer in return."

"Certainly, madam," he responded.

"Do not worry about my feelings. I am not hysterical, nor will I faint. I simply want to hear your real, real opinion."

"Upon what point?"

"In your heart of hearts do you think that Neville is alive?"

Sherlock seemed embarrassed by the question. "Frankly now!" she repeated.

"Frankly then, madam, I do not," he answered.

"You think that he is dead?"

"I do."

"Murdered?"

"I don't say that. Perhaps."

"And on what day did he meet his death?"

"On Monday."

"Then perhaps, Mr. Holmes, you will be good enough to explain how I received a letter from him today?"

Sherlock Holmes sprang out of his chair. "What!" he roared.

"Yes, today." She stood smiling at him and held up a letter.

"May I see it?" Holmes asked.

"Certainly."

He snatched it from her in his eagerness. Then he smoothed it out on the table, moved a lamp close to it and examined the envelope carefully. I left my chair and peered over his shoulder. The envelope was very plain. The date on the postmark was of that very day—or rather the day before, as it was now after midnight.

"Coarse writing!" murmured Holmes. "Surely this is not your husband's handwriting?"

"No, but the writing of the note within is."

"I see that whoever addressed the envelope had to go and ask about the address."

"How can you tell that?" she asked.

"The name is in perfectly black ink, which has dried by itself. The rest is a grayish color, showing that it was blotted dry. If the name and address had been written at once and blotted, it would all appear gray. No, this man wrote the name and then there was a pause before he wrote the address. This could only mean that he was not familiar with it. It is of course a small matter, but small matters often prove of great importance. Let us now see the letter! Ha! Something else was in this envelope."

"Yes, there was a ring. His signet ring," Mrs. St. Clair said.

"And you are sure this is your husband's handwriting?" Holmes asked again.

"One of his."

"One?" questioned Holmes.

"His handwriting when he writes hurriedly. It is very unlike his usual writing, but I know it well."

" 'Dearest,' " read Holmes, " 'do not be frightened. All will come out well. There is a huge error which it may take some time to correct. Wait in patience. —Neville.' Written in pencil on the flyleaf of a book," Holmes commented. "Posted today by a man with a dirty thumb. Ha! The flap has been gummed, I perceive, by a man who has been chewing tobacco. And you have no doubt that this is your husband's handwriting?"

"None," Mrs. St. Clair said. "Neville wrote those words."

"And they were posted today. Well, Mrs. St. Clair, the clouds lighten, though the danger is not yet over."

"But he must be alive, Mr. Holmes."

"Unless this is a clever forgery to put us on the wrong scent."

"No, no; it is, it is his very own writing!" she exclaimed.

"Very well. It may, however, have been written on Monday and only posted today."

"That is possible."

"If so, much may have happened in between," Holmes said.

"Oh, you must not discourage me, Mr. Holmes. I would sense if something evil had happened to him. Why, on the very day I last saw him he cut himself in the bedroom, and yet I sensed something had happened and rushed to him from the dining room. Do you think I could sense such a small thing and not know of his death?"

"I have seen too much of female intuition to disagree with you. Certainly this letter is a very strong piece of evidence in your favor. But if your husband is alive and able to write letters, why should he remain away from you?"

"I cannot imagine," she answered. "It is unthinkable."

"On Monday did he mention anything to you before leaving?" Holmes asked.

"No."

"And were you surprised to see him above that den?"

"Very much so."

"Was the window open?" Holmes asked.

"Yes," she answered.

"Then he might have called to you?"

"He might."

"But he only gave a cry."

"Yes."

"A call for help, you thought?"

"Yes. And he waved his hands," she added.

"But it might have been a cry of surprise. He might have thrown up his hands in astonishment at having seen you?"

"It is possible."

"And you thought he was pulled back?" Holmes asked.

"He disappeared so suddenly," she answered.

"He might have leaped back. You did not see anyone else in the room?"

"No, but this horrible man confessed to being there . . . and the owner was at the foot of the stairs."

"Quite so. From what you could see, did your husband have his ordinary clothes on?"

"He seemed to, but without his collar or tie. I distinctly saw his bare throat," Mrs. St. Clair said.

"Has he ever spoken of this den?"

"Never."

"Had he ever shown any signs of taking opium?"

"Never."

"Thank you, Mrs. St. Clair," Holmes said. "Those were the main points I wanted to be clear on. Now we shall have a little supper and then retire. Tomorrow may be a very busy day."

We were given a large and comfortable double-bedded room. It was not long before I was between the sheets. But Holmes could never sleep when a problem weighed upon his mind. He would spend days, or even weeks without rest, rearranging the facts in his mind. That night he changed into a blue dressing gown, and placed some pillows on the floor. There he sat, his pipe in his mouth, an ounce of tobacco in his lap, thinking about the case. When I awoke, the room was thick with smoke. The ounce of tobacco was gone and Holmes was still sitting in the same position I had seen him in last.

"Awake, Watson?" Holmes asked.

"Yes."

"Up for a morning drive?"

"Certainly," I said.

"Then dress. No one is stirring yet, but I know where the stable boy sleeps. We can soon have the carriage out." He chuckled to himself as he spoke. He seemed quite a different man from the serious thinker of the night before.

I glanced at my watch. No wonder no one was stirring. It was twenty-five minutes past four. I had hardly finished dressing when Holmes returned to say that the stable boy was taking out our horse.

"I want to test a little theory of mine," Holmes said as he pulled on his boots. "I think, Watson, that you are standing in the presence of one of Europe's greatest fools. I deserve to be kicked for having missed this one. But I think I have the key to the affair now."

"And where is it?" I asked, jokingly.

"In the bathroom," he answered. "No. I am not joking. I have just been there and found it. It is now in my carpetbag. Come on, my boy, we shall see whether it fits the lock."

We made our way downstairs as quietly as possible. Our horse and carriage stood waiting for us outside. We jumped in and away we dashed down the London road.

"It has been an unusual case," said Holmes as he flicked the horse into a gallop. "I confess that I have been as blind as a mole. Still, it is better to learn late, than not at all."

Holmes drove us back to London and directly to the police station. He was well-known on the force and two policemen saluted him as we pulled up. One took hold of our horse while the other led us into the station.

"Who is on duty?" asked Holmes.

"Inspector Bradstreet, sir."

"Ah, Bradstreet, how are you?" Holmes asked a tall, rather stout official who had just entered. "I wish to have a quiet word with you."

"Certainly, Mr. Holmes. Step into my room here."

We walked into a small officelike room nearby. The Inspector sat down at his desk.

"What can I do for you, Mr. Holmes?"

"I am here about the beggar, Boone—the one who was charged for being involved with the disappearance of Neville St. Clair of Lee."

"Yes. He is here in one of the cells."

"Is he quiet?" Holmes asked.

"Oh, he gives us no trouble. But he is a dirty scoundrel."

"Dirty?"

"We got him to wash his hands, but his face is as black as a chimney sweep's. Well, as soon as his case is settled we'll give him a proper prison bath. I think, if you saw him, you'd agree that he needed it!"

"I should like to see him very much," said Holmes.

"Would you? That is easily done. Come this way. You can leave your bag here," the Inspector said.

"No, I think I'll take it," answered Holmes.

"Very good. Come this way, if you please." The Inspector led us down a passage, beyond a barred door, down a winding staircase, and into a white-washed corridor with a line of doors on each side.

"The third on the right is his," he said. "Here it is!"

He quietly pushed back a panel in the upper part of the door and glanced through.

"He is asleep," the Inspector said. "You can see him very well."

We both peered through the panel. The prisoner lay with his face toward us. He was in a very deep sleep and his breathing was slow and heavy. He was a middle-sized man and was dressed coarsely as suited his profession. He was, as the Inspector had said, extremely dirty. But the grime on his face could not conceal its repulsive ugliness. A broad scar went right across his face from his eye to his chin. It twisted one side of his upper lip so that it looked as if he was snarling. His hair was bright orange.

"He's a beauty, isn't he?" said the Inspector.

"He certainly needs a wash," remarked Holmes. "I had an idea he might and so I brought the tools with me." He opened up his carpetbag and there was a very large bath sponge.

"Ha! Ha! You are a funny one," chuckled the Inspector.

"Now, if you will open the door very quietly, we will soon have him looking respectable."

"Well, I don't know why not," said the Inspector. "He's certainly no credit to our cells now." He slipped his key into the lock and we all entered the cell. The sleeper half turned, but settled down once more. Holmes stopped at the water jug and wet his sponge. Then he quickly rubbed it across and down the prisoner's face.

"Let me introduce you," he shouted, "to Mr. Neville St. Clair of Lee."

Never in my life have I seen such a sight. The man's face peeled off under the sponge just like the bark of a tree. Gone was the coarse brown tint! Gone, too, was the horrid scar and the repulsive twisted lip! One pull and the shock of hair came away as well. There, sitting up in bed, was a pale, sad-faced man with black hair and smooth skin. He rubbed his eyes and stared about him in confusion. Suddenly he realized that he had been found out. He let out a scream and threw himself face-down on the pillow.

"Great heavens!" cried the Inspector. "It is indeed the missing man. I know him from his photograph. I've been on the force for twenty-seven years, but this takes the cake!"

"If I am Mr. Neville St. Clair, then he has neither been kidnapped nor murdered," said the prisoner, "and no crime has been committed. I am therefore being held illegally."

"No crime, but a very great error has been committed," said Holmes. "You should have trusted your wife."

"It was not my wife I feared," groaned the prisoner, "I did not want my children to be ashamed of their own father. My God! What can I do? There will be much publicity now and they are bound to find out. They will have to go through life bearing my shame," the man cried.

Sherlock Holmes sat down beside him and patted him on the shoulder.

"You can hardly avoid publicity if the case goes to court," he said. "However, if you convince the police that there is no case against you, I do not see how it will reach the papers. I am sure Inspector Bradstreet could make notes on anything you tell us. He could then submit them to the proper authorities. The case would never go to court at all."

"God bless you!" cried the prisoner. "I would rather have endured imprisonment, even execution, than leave a blot on the family name.

"You are the first to hear my story. My father was a schoolmaster in Chesterfield and I received an excellent education. I traveled in my youth, worked for a while as an actor, and finally became a reporter on an evening paper in London. One day my editor wanted to publish a series of articles on begging. I volunteered to write them. This is how my adventure started. I decided I could best get the facts by posing as a beggar myself. As an actor I had learned the art of makeup. I painted my face and tried to make myself look as pitiable as possible. I made a good scar and fixed one side of my lip in a twist by using a small piece of plaster. Then I put on a red wig and found some tattered clothes. Dressed in this outfit, I went to the busiest part of the business district and posed as a beggar. I sat there for seven hours. When I returned home I was surprised to find that I had earned quite a bit of money.

"I wrote my articles and thought little more of the matter. But later I went into debt. I was at my wit's end as how to come up with the money. But then an idea came to me. I asked for a holiday from my employer and spent the time begging in the city. Within ten days I had the money and the debt was paid.

"Well, you can imagine how difficult it was to settle back down to work. I could earn as much in one day at begging as I earned in a week at my regular job. There was a fight between my pride and the money, but the money won out. At last I stopped reporting and sat day after day on Threadneedle Street. Only one man knew my secret.

He was the keeper of a low den called The Bar of Gold. There, I would change into my costume each morning and emerge as a beggar. In the evenings I would transform myself back into a well-dressed man about town. I paid the owner well for the use of his rooms, and so I knew my secret was safe.

"Well, very soon, I was saving considerable sums of money. I am not saying that every beggar in London can earn a fortune at his trade. But I am skilled in makeup and soon learned how to talk with the passersby. I became a recognized character. All day a stream of pennies, sometimes even silver, poured into my cap.

"As I grew richer, I grew more ambitious. I bought a house in the country and even married without anyone suspecting my real occupation. My dear wife knew I had business in the city. But she did not know what type.

"Last Monday I had just finished for the day. I was dressing in my room above the opium den. I looked out of the window and saw my wife. I was both astonished and horrified. She was standing below, looking straight up at me. I gave a cry of surprise and threw up my arms to cover my face. Then I rushed to the owner and begged him not to let anyone up. I heard my wife's voice downstairs, but I knew he would not let her up. I threw off my clothes and quickly made myself up into the beggar. Even a wife's eyes could not see through my disguise. But then it occurred to me that there might be a search of the room. My clothes would betray me. I threw open the back window and reopened a cut I had got that morning in my bedroom. I seized my coat. I had transferred my beggar's coins to its pockets and it was heavy. I hurled it out the window. It disappeared into the river below. I was going to throw out the rest, but at that moment the police rushed up the stairs. Instead of being recognized as Neville St. Clair, I was arrested as his murderer.

"I do not know if there is anything else to explain. I was determined to keep my disguise as long as possible. That is why I would not wash my face. I knew my wife was anxious. When I had a chance, I gave a letter to the owner of the den to mail. It contained my ring and a hasty note assuring her that I was all right."

"The letter only reached her yesterday," said Holmes.

"Good God!" St. Clair said. "What a week she must have spent."

"The police were watching the owner," Inspector Bradstreet said. "It was most likely difficult for him to mail it unobserved. He probably handed it to some sailor customer who forgot about it for a few days."

"That was it," said Holmes. "I have no doubt of it. But haven't you ever been fined for begging?"

"Many times, but I always paid the fine and they let me go."

"It must stop here, however," said Bradstreet. "If the police are to hush this thing up, there must be no more of Hugh Boone."

"I swear it most solemnly."

"In that case I think we can arrange it. But if you are found begging again, then all must come out into the open. Mr. Holmes, we are very much indebted to you for clearing the matter up. I wish I knew how you reached your results."

"I reached this one," said my friend, "by sitting on five pillows and smoking an ounce of tobacco. I think, Watson, that we should drive back to Baker Street. We should just be in time for breakfast."

BOOK THREE

Sir Arthur Conan Doyle's
THE ADVENTURES OF
SHERLOCK HOLMES

Adapted for young readers by Catherine Edwards Sadler

The Adventure of the Engineer's Thumb When a young engineer arrives in Dr. Watson's office with his thumb missing, it leads to a mystery in a secret mansion, and a ring of deadly criminals.

The Adventure of the Beryl Coronet Holmes is sure that an accused jewel thief is innocent, but will he be able to prove it?

The Adventure of Silver Blaze Where is Silver Blaze, a favored racehorse which has vanished before a big race?

The Adventure of the Musgrave Ritual A family ritual handed down from generation to generation seemed to be mere mumbo-jumbo—until a butler disappears and a house maid goes mad.

Join the uncanny and extraordinary Sherlock Holmes, and his friend and chronicler, Dr. Watson, as they tackle dangerous crimes and untangle the most intricate mysteries.

AVON **C** CAMELOT

**AN AVON CAMELOT ORIGINAL • $2.95 U.S./$3.50 Can.
(ISBN: 0-380-78105-0)**

BOOK FOUR

Sir Arthur Conan Doyle's
THE ADVENTURES OF
SHERLOCK HOLMES

Adapted for young readers by Catherine Edwards Sadler

The Adventure of the Reigate Puzzle Holmes comes near death to unravel a devilish case of murder and blackmail.

The Adventure of the Crooked Man The key to this strange mystery lies in the deadly secrets of a wicked man's past.

The Adventure of the Greek Interpreter Sherlock's brilliant older brother joins Holmes on the hunt for a bunch of ruthless villains in a case of kidnapping.

The Adventure of the Naval Treaty Only Holmes can untangle a case that threatens the national security of England, and becomes a matter of life and death.

Join the uncanny and extraordinary Sherlock Holmes, and his friend and chronicler Dr. Watson, as they tackle dangerous crimes and untangle the most intricate mysteries.

AVON CAMELOT

AN AVON CAMELOT ORIGINAL • $2.75 U.S./$3.75 Can.
(ISBN: 0-380-78113-1)